ALARM GIRL

ALARM GIRL

Hannah Vincent

Published in 2014 by

Myriad Editions
59 Lansdowne Place
Brighton BN3 1FL

www.myriadeditions.com

1 3 5 7 9 10 8 6 4 2

A CIP catalogue record for this book is available from the British Library.

ISBN: 978-1-908434-45-6

Printed and bound in Sweden
by ScandBook AB

To Bosie,
fellow traveller

AT THE BEGINNING the air was so thick I couldn't breathe it properly. When we got off the plane I had to hold on to the handrail like an old person. I was afraid my rucksack would tip me over. The air stewardess's shoes clanged on the metal steps and Robin told me to hurry up. We were walking so fast we had to run. Robin's arms were flapping and the light was so bright and glinty my eyes went weird. Through some doors it was suddenly as noisy as the swimming pool. A big crowd was pressed up against the barrier. There were posters for Nelson Mandela and a man was wearing a T-shirt with his face on. Another man in a suit was holding a piece of cardboard with a funny word that had lots of 'o's. A woman had a turban that made her the tallest out of everyone.

I saw Dad straight away but the stewardess kept going, whizzing our suitcases along on their noisy wheels with her high heels clicking and clacking. She looked like she would click-clack past all the people waiting, past Dad, and out the other side of the airport, keep on click-clacking until she came to the sea.

He was wearing a white T-shirt and a denim shirt over the top. The shirt was open and the T-shirt was so white it made his eyes look extra blue. It had the words Taylored Travel written on it. Luckily Robin couldn't tell I was crying, because we were both squashed up in his hug while he kissed us and pressed us into him and said Welcome to South Africa. Every time we see him I forget the smell of him, then I remember it again.

The stewardess wrote down the number of Dad's passport. He asked if she wanted his phone number as well and she laughed and tipped her head so far back you could see the edge of her make-up. He said What do you say, babies? I knew he wanted us to say thank you to her for looking after us, but I pretended not to understand. I said bye instead. Robin said Thanks for looking after us and the stewardess called him a gentleman but really he was just a bum-licker. It was very nice to meet you, Indy, she said, and I had to say Nice to meet you too. She said to Dad She's got quite a stare, hasn't she? She was talking about me. Then she said for us babies to have a good holiday and she was gone. Robin is twelve and I am ten and three-quarters. We are not babies.

On the way to the car park Dad asked if I wanted to take off my hoody. I told him it was cosy and he laughed. You want to be cosy, do you? In this heat? I couldn't see his eyes because he had sunglasses on. His car was bigger and posher than Grandad's but there were golf sticks in the boot that he forgot to take out so there was barely any room for our bags. They got shoved right in. Dad said What have you got in here, a dead body? Robin saw me twisting my scarf and I could tell he was annoyed. Dad gave the car park man some money and took the ticket off the man without saying anything, not even thank you. We drove away from the airport so fast my body felt like it was travelling too far forward for my brain to catch up. I had to shut my eyes until I came back all together again. You've had your hair cut, Indy, Dad said, and I said yes and he said it suited me short. Then he asked loads of questions, about the plane journey and about school, about our friends, about Christmas and about what we wanted to do while we were here. When he said How are Val and Doug he meant Nan and Grandad. Robin said Okay and nobody said anything after that.

Once I said to Nan Do you like Dad? She said Of course I like your dad, Indigo, he's your dad, isn't he? If I say something like that to Robin he tells me I'm shit-stirring and being a girl.

Soon there were lots of houses that all looked the same, and washing drying in the sun. Some was spread on the ground and on bushes. Nan wouldn't like that. Birds sat in a crowd on the top of a tree, like big white hankies, as if Nan had washed some of Grandad's and they got blown away by the wind. I saw some kids playing football, but not with a ball – with a clump of something all bundled up with string. They didn't wear shoes and some didn't have any tops on. Some wore T-shirts so big they reached down to their knees like dresses. Then there were falling-down sheds and Portaloos, all slanting among bits of metal and planks of wood. Dad and Robin were going on about football but Dad kept looking at me in the little rectangle of the driver's mirror so I closed my eyes. The sun flickered in stripes across my eyelids, bands of darkness in between the bright, like stripes of a zebra, stripes of wires criss-crossing the sky. The car engine hummed and I wished we could stay driving and never stop. Never stop and get out and walk and speak and live. Never do all the things Robin and Dad talked about doing, the things Dad had planned for us like shopping and surfing and football and safari, just stay driving with the sun flickering.

THE STADIUM WAS FILLED with extravagant costumes and painted faces. Ian turned up the volume on the television and the tiny living room filled with the noise of triumphant horns, vuvuzelas and drums.

'It's too loud, turn it down,' Indigo complained.

'It's the World Cup, Indy!' Ian cried above the din.

'It's the World Cup!' Robin shouted.

'I was having a nice peaceful time,' the little girl said, turning to Karen.

'I know, puppy,' Karen said. 'Show me what you've made.'

She had stuck an entire pack of sequins to a picture of a mermaid. The paper sagged, threatening to fall apart with the weight of the glue, and the mass of green and turquoise shiny discs caught the light, setting emerald and blue phantoms dancing across the living room walls.

'Beautiful,' Karen said, kissing her child's head and breathing in her biscuity smell.

'It's starting,' Ian said.

She joined him on the sofa. The commentator compared the atmosphere to the thrill of a child on Christmas morning.

'It makes me feel homesick,' she said. 'Homesick for Africa.' She lifted Ian's arm and placed it around her shoulder.

'You can't be homesick – it's not your home,' Robin said.

'No, you're right, I'm being silly,' she said.

Somewhere they had visited before the children were born came into her mind – a clearing among trees, not significant in any way, other than the fact that it occurred to her now, randomly, as they waited for a televised football tournament to begin. They had travelled to so many countries in the years before their marriage and, as much as she recalled the landmarks and monuments recommended in the guidebooks, it was these incidental places she remembered most often.

It was announced that Nelson Mandela was not at the ceremony.

'Oh no, that's tragic,' she said.

'What's tragic?' Indigo asked, not looking up from her picture.

'Nelson Mandela's grandaughter died in a car crash.'

'But what's *tragic*?'

'Tragic means something sad,' Ian said.

It was possible to forget how much children didn't know. When they were on holiday a few years ago,

Robin had thought they would be living forever in the cottage they had rented. He was only young, had no notion of holidays, and they hadn't realised they needed to explain what it was. There were probably countless misconceptions their children carried around with them.

Ian's weight against hers was comforting. His heartbeat tocked in his chest, signalling to her through the chamber of his body, reminding her of his constancy. She knew that some of the places they had travelled to would have changed, but it was possible there were others, like the clearing she remembered, that hadn't altered at all. What was happening when they passed through – light playing on leaves, insects moving around in grass – could be happening there now as they sat on their sofa far away.

She lifted her legs on to Ian's lap and he gathered her to him, like a bundle of sticks. Their children had inherited her tallness, their sleeves and trouser-legs always too short. The sight of Robin's skinny arms poking out of his nylon football shirt as he sat transfixed by the television drummers and dancers made her feel as if her heart might break. She had to work hard not to allow the feeling to skid out of control.

A passer-by glanced in at them through their front window, which opened directly on to the street. The movement startled her – it was a surprise that not everyone was watching the World Cup as they were. Her younger self would have been horrified by the scene. She had assumed her life would be more interesting than the life her parents lived and yet here she was, indoors on a sunny day in a terraced house in small-town England.

Images of South African wildlife flashed up on the screen.

'Definitely take the kids on safari one day,' Ian said.

'Definitely,' she said.

'Could buy some land out there, even,' Ian said.

'When our boat comes in, you mean?' Karen said. She stroked his head. His hair had grown curly during the years they had spent travelling but he wore it cut short now. There was some grey in it already.

'Our life assurance is worth a few hundred thousand,' he said. 'Maybe we could have some kind of accident.'

'Something not too bad but just bad enough,' she said.

'What are you two stupids talking about?' Indy asked, and Ian laughed, told her they were messing about.

'Can't you get cancer?' he whispered in Karen's ear, mock-romantic, and quiet enough so Indy couldn't hear.

Karen laughed. 'Can't you?' she said.

I HEARD YOUR VOICE calling my name but we were driving too fast for you to catch up and when I looked around you were nowhere to be seen. I tried to shout but my voice was swallowed and there was no sound. Beth and Minnie were running after the car, with Minnie barking and Beth laughing and shouting.

Then I woke up.

I don't know how long I was asleep, it could have been five minutes or it could have been ages, but probably it was a long time because my neck was aching. The car jumped and jolted. You weren't anywhere and it wasn't Beth I could hear laughing and shouting, it was a crowd of children. Robin was waving at them and the car wasn't gliding any more, it was bumping over rough ground. Dad was driving with his window open and one arm hanging out, trailing his fingers along the children's like he was in a rowing boat trickling his hand in the water. The land on either side was empty country with hills in the distance that looked like monsters sleeping on their sides. If they woke up and moved, all the land around them would slide off in a big heap of trees and bushes and road and car. The children wanted me to wind down my window. Dad was speaking African to them and his voice didn't sound like his, he sounded like me and Beth when we pretend to be foreign. Bobble magoosheela? Bibboo babboo ganoo.

There was no window-winder, but Dad saw me in his mirror and pressed a button in the front that made my window open automatically. The air from outside was really warm compared with inside the car. The children were shouting How are you! How are you! and sticking their hands in as they ran along. Dad was speaking in their language and Robin asked him what he was saying to them. Dad said he was telling them he would introduce us later. The road got so bumpy he had to use both hands to jerk the steering wheel. It was a track, really, not a road, all cobbled with bits of rock and stones. Up ahead was a white archway with a weird word written across it and a skinny man in a uniform standing next to it. There was barbed wire all tangled up on top of the wall. The car stopped in front of the arch and the children stayed behind, watching the gate open. The man said something to them and they turned around and went back in the direction they had come from, but walking slowly this time.

The car rolled through the gate, which closed behind us. In front was a low building that looked a bit like a ranch, white with a red tiled roof like the stable that went with the toy farm I had when I was little. There was a clump of trees surrounded by a circle of boulders painted white, and tyre marks in the dust around the trees. There were shutters on all the windows of the house that were closed, and there was a Christmas decoration of gold and silver leaves on the front door.

We parked in the shade of the trees and someone came out from around the back of the house. The person stood watching as we got out of the car. I couldn't see if it was a girl or a boy at first. Dad bowed when he opened the car door, making a joke that I was the Queen. My legs felt like they could snap after the journey and it was as warm as the boiler cupboard where Nan keeps the clean sheets. There was a tangy smell, the same as the smell of my bedroom when Beth ate an apple and the core fell down the side of my bed and stayed there for ages.

My throat was all dry and scratchy. I needed a drink of Coke, or something cold with loads of ice. My clothes were chilly from the car and the heat came creeping in, like tickling fingers.

The person moved closer and I could see it was a boy. He looked about the same age as me, with brown skin and a face as round as a doll's. He was standing really still. Dad said Let me introduce you to Robin and Indigo and the boy came nearer but still a little bit away from us. The shirt he was wearing was too big. It had patterns and shapes all over it – blue and red and green with lots of little black scratchy lines all over that made my eyes go funny. Dad's hand closed around the back of my neck and I looked across and saw he was holding Robin the same way, like we were a pair of puppets. He pushed us over to the boy, speaking African first, in his African voice, then English. He told the boy our names again and the boy said Hellohowareyou without a gap between any of the words. Then he said his name but even though he said it really slowly, like you're meant to speak in assembly, I couldn't understand it. Dad said it was Zami for short but that wasn't what the boy said.

Something ran in front of us. It was an animal with a pointy snout and tusks. Robin jumped behind me and grabbed my arm – he almost pulled me over. The animal ran around us in a circle, kicking up the dust. Dad said Don't panic, Mr Mannering. It trotted over to stand next to the boy. It was all bristly, with gingery grey hair that lifted up so you could see its black crinkly skin underneath. Its ears were quite big, and the exact shape of an animal's ear when you draw one. Robin asked what it was and Dad said bushpig. He said it wouldn't hurt us. His name is Tonyhog, the boy said, and his voice was softer than anyone else's I ever heard. Dad scratched the bushpig on its back and said it was called Tony after a colleague of his. It was a joke that stuck, he said, and so has he. Now he's part of the family.

Then Robin did something weird. He stepped forward and held out his hand for the boy to shake. Since when did Robin shake hands with people? One minute he was getting into trouble with Nan for finishing off the biscuits and the next he was shaking hands like a businessman. Everything felt like a big trick, and I suddenly thought that the aeroplane and the airport and even the bushpig could be fake and we were in a TV programme that Dad had arranged. There could be ginormous heaters hidden behind the hills we saw, keeping the air hot. Maybe Dad wasn't Dad at all, but an actor with a false face. Maybe you weren't really dead and you would come out of the house in a minute, laughing and crying at the same time.

IT WAS DISCONCERTING having Ian's face filling the computer screen in the corner of the room when he was miles away. Doug stood in the kitchen doorway, drying his hands with a tea towel. He wasn't certain if being able to see Ian meant that Ian could see him, but he noticed Valerie remove her apron and quickly hide it behind the sofa cushions so perhaps that meant that he could. Not so long ago video-phones had been the stuff of science fiction films, yet now they were a reality. A reality in their own living room, what was more. A few years ago they wouldn't have thought it possible. But then, Doug thought, there were a lot of things they wouldn't have thought possible a few years ago.

He wished they had been able to see and speak to Karen when she and Ian had been travelling. It would have made a difference. When she'd got home there had been a distance between them that perhaps wouldn't have been there if she had been able to Skype them from India and Kenya and all the other places she had been. It was no use thinking like that, though, he told himself. That was before they'd had a computer, before anyone had thought of communicating in that way. In those days you were grateful if you got a postcard. They had kept her letters and photographs. When he was alone in the house, which wasn't that often now the kids were living with them, he went up into the attic to look through them. It was a bit like having a conversation with her. Valerie had scolded him the last time she came back from the shops and found the loft hatch open, asking what he thought would happen if he had a fall without her there to hold the ladder. 'What were you doing up there, anyhow?' she'd asked. He'd told her he thought he heard mice.

The doorbell rang.

'It's Beth,' Indigo told her dad, and she got up to answer the front door, nudging her brother with her foot on her way out of the room. Robin took her place at the computer, like the Changing of the Guard.

'Alright, Robbo?' Ian said.

'Alright, Dad.'

Indy came back into the room with her friend from next door.

'Is that another new pair of trainers, Bethany?' Val asked, forcing the poor girl to give an account of herself. She was too hard on her, Doug thought, but Val's comeback whenever he told her so was that there were plenty of ways to enjoy yourself that didn't cost the earth and to spare a thought for Beth's father working long hours to keep her in the latest fashions.

Beth had brought crisps and Coke to share while they watched television. Doug hoped they wouldn't want to use the phone to vote. When Robin finished speaking with Ian they all waved goodbye and the computer burped quietly as it swallowed his image – and the South African evening with it.

As usual, Robin came away from his conversation in a bad mood, complaining when he wasn't allowed to watch a film on the other channel. He declared the talent show participants 'a bunch of freaks' and accused his sister and her friend of being the same. There was always a change of atmosphere after Ian called. An argument erupted during which fizzy drink and crisps spilled all over the carpet.

'Fetch a cloth, Robbie,' Doug said.

Robin slammed the door as he left the room, making the walls of the house shake.

It grew late. Outside, a frost tightened the lawn. Votes were counted and television talent show winners announced.

'Isn't it about time you went home, Bethany?' Valerie said.

'Mum says she doesn't mind,' Beth answered without turning around.

Valerie gave Doug a look.

'Is she asleep?' he asked, nodding in Indigo's direction. Her head was cocked at an awkward angle over the arm of the chair, her hair falling in front of her eyes. She had done the same the previous weekend: dropped off to sleep while they were all watching television. They hadn't been able to wake her, no matter how hard they tried, no matter how loud they said her name and told her the house was on fire.

'Let's put stuff on her,' Robin said. He balanced the remote control on his sister's shoulder and Beth rested a cushion on top of her head. They put an orange from the fruit bowl into one of her hands, a banana in her lap.

'That's enough now,' Valerie said.

Doug removed the items and scooped his sleeping grandchild into his arms. His chest tightened painfully as he lifted her out of the armchair.

'Robin, mind out of Grandad's way,' Valerie said, 'or you'll have him break his neck.'

'She'll want this,' Robin said, holding up a silk scarf that Indigo always kept with her. Doug had no spare hand with which to take it so Robin tucked it under his sister's chin.

'Ah,' Beth said, 'pretend you're so hard, Robin Taylor, but you're a softie really.'

DAD'S BUNCH OF KEYS was as big as the school caretaker's. Nobody move, he said, when he opened the front door. Like the police. He told us to stay where we were while he turned off the alarm. I was fiddling with my scarf and Robin whispered at me not to be a retard. After Dad pressed loads of buttons we were allowed to go in.

It was dark and cool and smelled of polish. A vase of golden twigs stood on a chest made of wood that had all carvings on it and there was a big painting that was just colours but had people carrying spears if you looked at it more carefully. The front door opened straight into a big sitting room, with a shiny kitchen in the corner – no stairs or hallway or carpet. A Christmas tree had loads of presents underneath. It didn't feel like Christmas though because it was hot and sunny outside. Some big wide steps went down to two sofas opposite each other and a low table in the middle with a laptop on it and books and magazines, like at the dentist's. Dad went over and yanked a string that opened the curtains with a loud noise. The room filled with light. I recognised it from when we Skype except it looked different now we were standing in it. The whole back wall was a window. There was a big telescope in front of it and outside there was nothing apart from countryside. It didn't look like Africa because it was green not desert. It looked the same as England apart from the mountains. Robin looked through the telescope and said it was awesome.

I felt a bit dizzy. I really wanted a drink but it would be bad manners to ask for one. I held my scarf up to my face. It smelled of Nan's. Dad asked if I was alright but my throat swelled up fat enough to choke so I couldn't say anything and Dad gave me a weird look. He started showing us around and you could tell he was trying to make everything friendly. A news programme came on the massive TV screen on the wall above the fireplace. Dad pressed another button and random music filled the room. He called the kitchen bit the cooking station. The 'cooking station' was about four times the size of Nan's kitchen. He said we would have a chef and, if there was anything we fancied, just shout. I wanted to scream out loud for a drink but Robin started going on about how rich Dad was. Dad laughed and pretended to be embarrassed but you could tell he was pleased. He said we could either sleep in a round house where his clients normally stay or we could sleep in the main house with him if we preferred. Robin said he wanted to stay in the main house and I did too. It's not like we're his clients.

Our bedrooms were next door to each other but not upstairs. There were no stairs. There was an animal skull with horns on it hanging on the wall. Dad said to Robin How about you have this room and Indy can go in here? The bed had a long white net hanging around it, like a princess's bed. There were bars on the window, like in a prison. Dad said there wasn't such a good view from this part of the house. We could see the boy called Zami walking away from where he had parked Dad's car. It was next to an open-top Jeep under a shelter that had a roof but no walls, and the roof was a bit of metal held up by four knobbly posts that looked like they had been cut from trees. There were some chickens pecking the ground and some more lying under a shed and there was a kennel with a massive dog inside, about twenty times the size of Minnie and not too friendly, Dad said. It was tied to a long chain. No wonder it wasn't friendly. We carried on watching out of the window and Tonyhog trotted past with his tail pointing right up into the air in a straight line. Dad laughed and said Tony, on the other hand, is very keen to be friends. Ugly as hell, but he's good fun, you'll like him. We watched as Zami poured water out of a dirty plastic container and made a puddle that was for Tony to drink. Tonyhog knelt down with just his front legs bent underneath him. I was so thirsty I wanted to kneel down next to him. He wasn't ugly. He looked really sweet with his front legs tucked underneath the way humans fold their arms. I asked what the dog's name was but Dad said it liked to be left alone. He said there were a few house rules to go over – Stuff you need to know to keep you safe, he said – but we would talk about that after we unpacked.

On my pillow there was a thing that looked like a bit like a phone. It wasn't a phone, it was a personal alarm. Dad said Robin had one too so he went and got it. Mine was called Alarm Girl and it was silver and pink. Robin's was blue. They had inbuilt torches and a clip to fix them to your belt or you could wear them on a string around your neck like the glow sticks we got from the circus. If you take the pin out there's a horrible noise. Robin was making jokes, pretending to pull out the pin then throw it like a hand grenade. He kept shouting Cover! and diving under my bed and making Dad laugh. I wanted to hear what the alarm sounded like but Dad went all serious and said Not now, Indy, it's not a toy, it's for if you're in danger, but I kept asking and then he let me. I pulled out the pin like in the instructions and a girl started screaming. When I put the pin back in, she stopped. Robin tried his but it was a siren instead of a girl screaming. I wanted the siren one but Dad said I had to have the girl. Robin said more people come to your rescue if there's a girl or a woman screaming. Maybe that made him think Dad loves me more than him because he made me keep the screaming girl.

Dad's got a gun that gives an electric shock but he wouldn't let us see it even though Robin really wanted to. He got it because he was mugged and his wallet and everything was stolen so after that he got a stun gun. He could have got a real gun but he only wanted a stun one. Robin asked if Dad's mugger was a black man and Dad said yes this man was black but when he was burgled in England that robber was a white person. Dad said there's always a reason why people behave the way they do but there's no reason why Robin loved the idea of that stun gun so much, he just did.

Our rooms had ceiling fans like old-fashioned aeroplane propellers that moved slowly when you switched them on then they got faster and faster. The curtains around my bed blew and billowed. Dad asked if we were hungry. Starving, Robin said – like he always says if anyone asks – and I said I was thirsty. Dad said he would make pancakes and get me a drink.

I spread my scarf out over the little table next to the bed, smoothing its lovely silk and tracing the pattern of the golden letters. P.A.R.I.S. I said to Dad Do you remember this scarf? It was in the dressing-up box when we were little. He didn't remember it. I told him it was yours and he sat on my bed next to me and asked me what I thought of South Africa so far. It's a big country, he said, and sometimes it can feel overwhelming. The landscape and the heat, he said, sometimes it can feel too much – even I feel it. I didn't say anything. I knew he wasn't talking about Africa. I just wanted him to get my drink. We looked at my wind-up torch that doesn't need batteries. Dad said it never gets dark because of the security lights. We would need a torch if we went out at night, because it's pitch-black twenty metres away from the house with ridges we could fall down, but inside the grounds it's light the whole time. Robin said I would be pleased about that because I was scared of the dark. He said I was scared of everything – creepy-crawlies, lions, everything – and he told Dad I have to have the hall light on at home and I have to have my scarf wherever I go, like a baby with its blanket. When I shouted Fuck off at him Dad was nice and made him go out of my room. He went out too, so he could make pancakes and so I could have a bit of time to myself, he said.

My suitcase zip made a loud noise. Nan had folded all my clothes in neat squares. Tops in one pile and bottoms separate. Socks and knickers in the special bags she got from her catalogue. Everything was cold, like it had been in the fridge. My new sandals were all squashed. They still smelled of the shop and I had to peel the stickers off the bottoms. I got changed and my clothes felt nice and cool.

They gave us colouring books on the plane. Really babyish. Robin left his on the seat but I brought mine. The picture on the first page was of a bunch of flowers. The crayons that came with it were all melty from the heat. There were two different greens to colour in the flower stalks, dark and light. I made sure I didn't get the floor or the bed dirty with the little bits that came off. I brushed them into the drawer of the table next to my bed. There was a Bible inside, with a silver cross on the front and really thin pages. I could hear Dad speaking on the phone. He had forgotten my drink and I was afraid I would die from thirst.

I went into Robin's room where he was arranging his wildlife books, lining them up on top of his table. Dad's trying to get us to like everything isn't he, I said, and Robin told me to lighten up. He had a Bible in his drawer too. I asked him what we were meant to do with them and he said Pray, even though he doesn't believe in God or Heaven. Then Dad brought us water with ice cubes in. He had no shoes on, and instead of his trousers he was wearing a piece of material wrapped around like a skirt. A leather string around his neck had a pointy tooth hanging off. He said it was a Great White's. I didn't believe him but I didn't say anything. I drank my water so quickly it was painful. Robin hadn't even started his and mine was all gone. Dad asked if I wanted another one but I could hardly speak with the ice-cold all around my heart. He took my empty glass and you could see his bare footprints on the floor, walking out of the door.

The pancakes had chocolate sauce and pineapple. I sat on one of the high stools to eat mine and there were cloth napkins, like in a restaurant. Dad never used a napkin at home, only kitchen roll if he needed to wipe his mouth or something. When Robin's pancake was ready Dad let me bang a little gong. The end of the beater was wrapped in cloth. The sound it made was loud and soft at the same time, and kind of rippled through the air so you could almost see the airwaves.

I was wearing my T-shirt with the horse on it and Dad said On a horse you can get up close to the animals because they can only smell the horse so they don't know you're there. I said It's Robin who wants to see all the animals and Dad said What are you into these days? I said I didn't know.

I checked out the presents underneath the Christmas tree. The tree was fake like Nan's, except silver instead of realistic and only gold decorations, not multicoloured like Nan's. All the presents underneath were wrapped in silver wrapping paper with yellow ribbon tied around them and tags made from plain card with no pictures on, just our names written in old-fashioned ink pen. To Indigo with love. It didn't say who from. The handwriting wasn't Dad's. It was like the writing on an ancient manuscript that gets found in a grave in one of the films that Robin likes. There was a present for Dad, with his name written on the tag like all the others. When I asked him if he wrapped them up he said he wasn't very good at that kind of thing so I asked him who did but instead of telling me he said it was elves.

He got his big load of keys and showed us behind the house where the garden was and where there was a little round cottage for guests who come on holiday. It's got a thatched roof that looks like a pointy hat and inside the ceiling is a dome. It's the exact same shape as a beehive so now I know what a bee feels like. Next to the cottage there was a giant hole for a swimming pool. Robin jumped in, even though there was no water because the swimming pool wasn't made yet. Dad was laughing because he was doing front crawl up and down with no water and showing him his butterfly and backstroke.

The earth inside the hole wasn't brown like in Grandad's flowerbeds. If you were drawing it you would have to add red to the brown to get the right colour. Next time we come the hole will be a swimming pool and we can swim in it, and there are going to be some seats under the shade of a big tree, but for now there's a tyre swing. Dad made it specially for us so we had a go. I got black stuff all over my hands from the tyre but it was insane. Dad pushed us really high and it was my best moment so far.

Night-time came with no warning. We were on the tyre for ages and it was sunny and hot then suddenly it was dark and even a little bit cold. I didn't know Africa could be cold. Dad said it's because there are no clouds to keep the air warm. This was the time of day the mozzies get busy so we had to go indoors and put long sleeves on.

There was a black man in the kitchen. He had a knife. I hid behind Dad and that made him laugh – No need to be shy, Indy, he said, this is Silumko, our wonderful chef. Silumko was chopping vegetables. He didn't say anything, he just smiled. Dad said we were having shepherd's pie for dinner. He knows shepherd's pie is Robin's favourite. He lit some candles that smelled of lemons and he said if we listened carefully we might hear lions. Some were nearby and we could go out to see them. He didn't mean straight away, he meant the next day. I was glad we didn't have to go on safari right then. There was a giant bowl of crisps on the table. I wanted one but no one else was eating any, not even Robin and he loves crisps. When I took one it tasted of soap. I spat it out and I was quickly going to hide it but Dad saw me. He laughed and said to Silumko that I was so hungry I was eating pot-pourri.

After dinner, instead of just leaving us to go to bed by ourselves like Nan does, Dad came in to our rooms to say goodnight. He saw my malaria pills on the little table and he got annoyed with Nan because there's no malaria at his house and those pills were too strong, he said. They can make you crazy. He asked where Nan got them and when I said she ordered them online because she was scared of us getting malaria he was angry because he already told Nan the last time we Skyped that we didn't need them. I was going to ask if we could Skype Nan and Grandad to say we had arrived like Dad said we could and to say night-night but because he was in a bad mood I didn't.

Dogs were barking in the distance but not our one. Dad said he would only bark if there was an intruder. I put my Alarm Girl under my pillow and Dad said the guard that stands outside the gate would let us know if there was anyone trying to get in. Plus the tangled-up barbed wire, plus the burglar alarm that automatically contacts the police who come straight away.

I couldn't get to sleep. The TV was on but Dad wasn't watching it. He was talking on the phone to someone. I heard him telling whoever it was about my malaria medicine but it wasn't Nan he was speaking to because I know he doesn't speak in that kind of voice to her. When he saw me in the doorway he told whoever it was that he would ring them back. Can't sleep, treasure, he said, and I said I thought it was a shame the dog didn't have a name. He laughed and asked me if that was what was keeping me awake and I could think of a name for him if I liked. I said How about Jack and Dad said that was a nice name, it suits him because he is a rough and tough kind of dog. Dad said Are there any boys in your class called Jack and I said No. Then I went back to bed. Robin was pretending to be asleep when I went past his room but he knew I was standing there and when he started talking it made me jump. He said he hoped I wasn't going to be like this the whole time. Like what, I said. All weird, Robin said, and I said I hoped *he* wasn't going to be like *this* the whole time and when he asked Like what I said All mean.

Then I went into my own room and I fell asleep with lions and mosquitoes and muggers all around.

VALERIE WAS AT HER BEDROOM window when she saw Ian's car draw up. It wasn't the blue saloon he normally drove, it was a big shiny grey thing. She moved away from the window.

There was no answer when she knocked on Robin's door. He was lying on his bed with his eyes closed. He was so tall now that his feet hung off its end. He had headphones on, so she had to tap him on the leg to tell him his dad had arrived.

Downstairs, a dining chair lay upturned on a sheet of newspaper in the middle of the room.

'Almost there,' Doug said.

She opened the front door to her son-in-law, who kissed her hello. Sometimes there was no kiss. During the worst times there was none.

'Bit of DIY, Doug?' Ian asked by way of a greeting.

'You could say that,' Doug replied. 'I've already had a go at the table.'

Ian complimented him on the good job he was doing but she could tell he thought the old man had gone gaga. He probably imagined Doug was so bored in retirement that this was how he filled his days.

She made a pot of tea and, together with the children, they sat around the table. Ian rarely chose to sit on the sofa when he was at theirs, as if he was on business. In fact there was often some kind of business to attend to – school permission slips and money the children needed for something or other.

'How's it all going?' she asked, and he told them about paying guests he took golfing and on vineyard tours.

'Well, you're looking good on it, Ian,' she said.

He thanked her and seemed a little embarrassed. The bangle he wore slid down his arm as he pushed his hair back. It used to be Karen's. His hair was mostly grey now, but longer than before and curly like it was when they first knew him. It was true he looked well. Everyone looked better with a tan.

'And the lifestyle out there – you like it?' she asked.

'It's wonderful, Val. The climate, the landscape, being in the open. You'll have to come and see for yourself, won't she, Indy?' He stroked his daughter's cheek with his own and Indy complained that his felt prickly. She was too old, really, Valerie thought, to sit on her father's lap. She caught herself feeling bad that she hadn't been touchy-feely like that with Karen.

Ian said he wouldn't stop for dinner. She knew he preferred to get straight off so she had made sure the children were ready. He was always in a rush, as if he couldn't stand to be in their company.

'How d'you like the new car?' he asked as they stood all together on the pavement.

'Very swish,' she said. 'Is it a people-carrier?'

'Yes, for carrying the peeps.'

He was certainly in an upbeat mood – the most upbeat she had seen him lately. Robin asked if it was a hire car and Ian told him that no, he had bought it. He showed them the drinks-holder and the stereo. She wondered how he managed to afford a new car on top of all the travel backwards and forwards to South Africa. His business must be doing as well as he said it was.

'What do you say, babies?' he asked.

She wished he wouldn't make them thank her for having them. It wasn't that she didn't appreciate good manners, but it made things too formal.

'Thanks for having us,' Robin said.

Ian promised to bring them back at the weekend and he made a point, as he always did, of telling her and Doug that they were welcome to come to the house. There were too many reminders, though, in the fairy-lights strung around the kitchen window frame, in sofa cushions that still smelled of her.

She waved goodbye to the disappearing car, and kept waving because Indy continued to stare at them out of the back window. 'Keep waving, Doug, she's still looking.' They waved until her face faded into a pale oval and even then they carried on waving, until they saw the indicator blinking and the brake lights come on at the junction at the bottom of the hill. Then the car pulled away, out of sight.

Later that evening, eating a bar of fruit-and-nut while Doug dozed in front of the television, Valerie noticed a series of minuscule felt-tipped hearts drawn along the windowsill, like a parade of ants. They continued their journey across the wall and on to the television cabinet. She gave her husband a gentle nudge but when he didn't wake up she had to poke him quite hard.

'Doug,' she said, 'you missed some.'

A DOG WAS BARKING and a cock was crowing. The shape of a helicopter's propeller was printed on the insides of my eyelids. I opened my eyes and saw the ceiling fan.

It was morning even though I didn't know I had been asleep. I felt warm and cold at the same time and I knew what that meant. The cold was my pyjama bottoms sticking to my legs. It hadn't happened in ages.

I crouched down next to the bed like a ninja and pulled the sheet off. The mattress didn't look too bad. I changed my pyjama bottoms for dry ones. Luckily I had two pairs. There was a shushing noise coming from outside and a hissing, like air escaping from a tyre. A dog was still barking, but not Jack – one further away. It was already hot outside when I opened the shutters. The sun was so bright it was blinding and the air pressed in like a fat, warm pillow. I had a glass of water left over from the night, so I held the pissy sheet and bottoms through the bars of the window and poured it all over them. I left them hanging there so they would dry. The chickens were out from underneath the cars and the shushing sound was Zami with a broom, sweeping the yard. He had bare feet and a piece of material wrapped around him like a skirt, the same as Dad. He was wearing a T-shirt with the cloth skirt, not bare like Dad. I stood to one side of the shutter so he wouldn't see me and I watched him sweeping and sweeping with the chickens following him, pecking. He collected up all the small sticks and leaves and dust on a square of cardboard and carried them over to the fence, where he tipped them on to a pile. Then he picked up his broom again and kept on sweeping.

Page two in the aeroplane drawing book was a picture of a clown. I coloured his hair in yellow and his shoes in red. The spots on his costume were blue and green. I heard the television go on so I went to my door and listened. I could see into Robin's room. He was still asleep. I crept in and put my face right next to his. I couldn't hear air going in or out and his chest wasn't going up and down but his mouth was open and his breath stank so bad I could tell he was alive. I went out again.

Dad was sitting on one of the sofas watching the news. He wasn't wearing any clothes apart from his sarong thing and nothing else except his shark-tooth necklace. His chest was quite hairy. He said Good morning, treasure and asked me how did I sleep. I never know what to say when people ask that – everyone sleeps the same. He called me puppy and gave me a cuddle and apart from his shark-tooth necklace for about two seconds it was like you were right there in the room. He never used to wear a necklace. I said Swear on mine and Robin's lives that's a Great White's tooth and he said I swear so it must be.

For breakfast Silumko was making eggy bread or there was fruit salad. I said I wanted cereal and Dad said What kind? Any kind, I said. Dad said you can get anything you want in South Africa.

Silumko lives in the village with his wife and daughter and baby boy. He supports the same football team as Dad. His daughter's name means 'blessing' in his language. Dad made a joke about fathers loving their daughters and having to protect them – from rascals who would pinch them, he said. He said it was a terrible thing to have a daughter but he was smiling when he said it, like it was a joke. Silumko said You are right, man. Dad said I know it, man. He told me I was growing up into a young lady and that I wasn't a girl any more. I said it was nice for Silumko to live at home with his daughter and Dad said he was working hard so one day me and Robin could come and join him and live here. I didn't say anything but secretly I was thinking I wouldn't like to live in South Africa and when would I see Beth and who would look after Nan and Grandad? Zami lives in a concrete building in the yard next to where the cars are parked. Me and Robin would have to live in a place like that because the proper rooms are for guests.

Dad said the big town nearby had nice girlie shops. He was telling me all the things there were to do but in my mind I just wanted to go on the tyre swing. Zami came in and Tony the bushpig was following him with his hooves going tap-tap on the floor. Zami gave Dad some letters and a newspaper. Silumko said something in a foreign language and Dad told Zami to take Tony out into the garden and why didn't I go with them too.

I was still wearing my pyjamas but I had my sun cream on like Nan told me to every time we are outside. The dusty ground felt like sand under my bare feet. I asked Zami if there were any snakes. Robin says African ones are deadly but I know he's trying to wind me up. Tony walked next to me, like he was trying to keep the same pace as me. He was keeping me company. He looked like he was walking on tiptoe. His hooves were like miniature high heels. He let me touch him. His skin was all rough.

I could hear hissing, louder than before. I said to Zami Are you sure there aren't any snakes but it wasn't a snake. It was coming from all around. Zami couldn't hear anything. His voice was so quiet I had to ask him to say everything twice, like I was deaf with just hissing in my ears. Like Grandad's before the wax got taken out. Zami got the water container and poured some water into the same bit of dust as before. He did it in silence with me following him. He swirled the water around with a stick and then he spoke without me asking him a question. To make it good for him to bathe in when it is hot in the day, he said. When he speaks he sounds like someone in a history book and his face is a perfect circle.

Tonyhog lay down in the mud that Zami made. His legs stuck out from his body straight as twigs. Me and Zami were scratching his back and the top of his head. Dad's garden has got giant weird cactus plants all around and the grass is really green and like velvet but near the Jeep the ground is bare. I left my sandals by the tyre swing all night but I could only find one and it was half destroyed. Only the sole and one strap with its buckle was left. Zami said jackals ate it but I didn't believe him and I didn't even know what jackals were. When I went back in the house, Robin was stuffing his face and talking with Dad and Silumko about football. Dad said What's the matter, Indy, you look as if you've seen a ghost but he meant my sun cream. I showed them my broken sandal and Dad said jackals are a kind of fox who come right up to the house at night. Once they tore the seats of his Jeep with their claws and tried to eat the leather. He said it was true what Zami said and they probably did eat my sandals. Don't be upset, Indy, he said, because I was crying. We can go shopping and get you a pair of South African shoes. That made Robin think I was a spoilt brat and he told me to go and wash my hands because I had been touching wild animals, meaning Tonyhog. I said Tony's not wild, he's tame and Robin said He's still got germs and Dad said he was right I should wash my hands.

Even though Robin's got loads of animal books, he only wants to know facts about them instead of actually liking them.

No one knew what I was talking about when I asked what the hissing noise was. I made them listen but none of them could hear it. Robin said it could be insects or a hosepipe watering the grass but Dad said That, my puppy, is the hiss of life itself. I had my scarf and Robin told him Nan and Grandad's name for me, Mrs Fiddle. Dad said he wished they wouldn't call me that, as if he knew it already. Then Robin said about me drawing on Nan and Grandad's furniture. Dad didn't know about that. Probably Nan didn't even tell him. I told him I didn't draw much and Nan didn't mind but it wasn't true, she did mind. I drew hearts on the table legs with black pen that wouldn't come off so Grandad had to get his toolbox out and sandpaper them. I drew hearts on the top of the table too and on the wall. Robin told Dad how Grandad had to sand everything then varnish it to get rid of the pen. Dad was shocked, but he was laughing. Robin tried to get me into trouble by saying Nan was really angry but it didn't work, Dad thought it was funny, so Robin got annoyed and started moaning how no one ever tells me off. He called me Indy, but in a baby voice so I could tell he was being mean.

It's true Nan didn't tell me off much about drawing on the furniture. Not as much as you would think. Her and Grandad just looked at me with sad faces and asked why I would do such a thing. I told them it was because I couldn't find any paper, which wasn't true. I had loads of paper. I don't know why I did it. I liked the shape of the hearts I was drawing, all round and fat and going to a sharp point, and once I started I couldn't stop.

Dad showed me a picture of a jackal on his laptop. It was a sort of fox but with a mean face. When I was washing my hands to get rid of Tony's wild animal germs I sneaked into Dad's room. It was the same as mine and Robin's, all plain with nothing in it apart from a wardrobe, but it smelled different and there was a painting on the wall like the one in the hallways. It looks like blobs of paint until you notice it's really a woman carrying a spear. The mosquito net over the bed was tied in a knot and hanging all bundled up from the ceiling. It looked like something fat in a cocoon that was just about to get born. There were some necklaces hanging on the wardrobe door handle and a key in the little lock. I ran the beads through my fingers. The air was all perfumey and I started to get a headache. The key turned easily and the necklaces clattered against the wardrobe door when I opened it. Inside were skirts and dresses and tops. Lots were white and there were some turquoise things and some patterned, but mostly white. I didn't recognise them. They weren't yours. At the bottom was a jumble of shoes – some old trainers and walking boots as well as a pair of gold plaited sandals. I knew I should stop being nosy but my legs wouldn't move. The flowery smell put me in a hypnotist's trance. I felt like Snow White when she eats the apple and faints. There was a mirror on the inside of the wardrobe door and my face in it was like a dead person's, all white from my sun cream. If I forget what you looked like I look at my own face in the mirror and I can remember. Now I stared at my face in Dad's mirror and I showed my teeth and growled. I didn't look like you any more. My eyes were all narrow and I was vicious, like a jackal that could tear the clothes hanging in the wardrobe to pieces and toss the shoes all about. Rip big holes in the mosquito net and roll around on the bed, covering everything with my oniony jackal smell. I snarled at my reflection. If they could do that to a pair of sandals or a car seat, imagine what they could do to a human.

I shut the wardrobe door and turned the little key in its lock.

The person Zami likes best is Tonyhog, even though he's not a person. After that he likes Lindisizwe who guards the gate. Lindisizwe stands up all day and all night. Dad showed me how to write his name and Zami's proper name, which is Z.a.m.i.k.h.a.y.a. When he's not guarding, Lindisizwe lives in the village which is the same one where Silumko lives. Dad took us there. There weren't any shops but there was a shack where you could buy Coke. There were posters for Nelson Mandela with the dates of his life on and his nickname, not his real name. Some chickens were pecking the ground and some dogs were in the shade. Robin played football and me and Zami watched. Dad said football is a universal language. I didn't know what that meant. We watched and we drank Coke. Dad bought some for the other kids too. One of the boys had trainers on, but two different ones that didn't match. The others had bare feet and all of their clothes were old. Dad asked one of the mothers to plait my hair but it was too short to do it properly and my ears were sticking out and Robin called me a bald eagle so I took the plaits out when we got back.

Before dark, the living room at Dad's was full of pink sunset. Dad made us put on our insect repellent for playing on the tyre swing. I remembered to bring my shoes inside the house this time. Robin was feeling ill but when I said he might have malaria he got annoyed and wanted me to leave him alone. If we caught malaria and died Dad would be an orphan as well as a widow. Dad said probably swinging on the tyre made Robin dizzy and that was why he was feeling ill. He made him drink lots of water because he had been running around playing football. I didn't want to drink too much because of the night and because of the feeling of waking up and moving my legs under the sheet, waiting to see if it sticks, waiting for the warm to turn cold. The best is when I kick my feet and the sheet goes upwards and falls softly down like a parachute.

Before we went to bed I put Dad's Christmas present under the fake tree. Robin thought I was looking at the presents which made him call me a spoilt brat but I wasn't looking at the presents, I was looking at the writing on the presents. I said to Robin Do you think he's going to talk to us about Mum? Robin said Shut the fuck up but he whispered it and I could tell he was thinking the same as me, which was Dad was going to give us a talk about you. That was why he made us come here instead of him coming to England like usual.

Whenever I ask Robin why no one in our family talks about you he says it's too sad and we probably wouldn't understand that's why. I say Of course it's sad when your Mum dies, that doesn't mean you can't talk about her, but then he just says Not everyone is like you, Indigo and Don't be so selfish. He is glad we don't see the bereavement counsellor any more. He said what was the point doing graffiti on a special graffiti wall, the whole point of graffiti is that it's on a proper wall, hopefully someone else's or the wall of a school or something. He said the other kids at grief counselling were nerds. The place we did it is too far to travel from Nan and Grandad's house anyway so we only go when we feel like it which is never. I liked writing to you on a balloon though, and the bereavement counsellor was the only person who liked me talking about you. Robin said she was a Goth but she wasn't, she just wore black nail varnish sometimes.

In the morning we had to get up really early, so early it was dark. Dad was taking us on a game drive. Not a game you play. I didn't feel like driving anywhere, though, so I started the next colouring-in. The picture was of a hot-air balloon and I coloured in a red section, a pink section, an orange section and a yellow section and then because it looked like the sunset I started colouring in the sky all around it in stripes of the same colours. Dad told me off for not being ready. Everyone was waiting and Dad was jingling his keys but I wanted Cookie Crisp. Robin had seconds, which Nan wouldn't agree with because she says sugary cereal puts him in a bad mood.

I didn't want to go on a drive so I asked if I could stay at the house by myself. Dad said Oh, come on, Indigo, you're in Africa, you can see animals here you would never get to see at home. I said My favourite animals are dogs and you get loads of them in England. Dad made a joke that next time he comes back me and Robin can take him on safari too but I said When are you coming then? That made him stop laughing. After we finished our cereal he told us to stand outside while he set the alarm. Robin gave me a dig so hard I could feel it turning into a bruise straight away.

Zami was waiting next to the Jeep. I didn't know he was coming and I was glad it wasn't just me and stupid Robin. The Jeep smelled of petrol and its seats were torn up, with stuffing poking through. It was all spongey and good to pick but I had to hide the pile I made in case I got told off. There were no car windows, just a material roof to roll down if it rained. Me and Zami sat in the back. He saw me picking the seat stuffing but he didn't say anything. It was freezing cold so we had a blanket. Dad had to start the engine by lifting up the bonnet. It made a loud noise and loads of smoke and smell. Lindisizwe was standing outside as usual. He never goes to sleep. Instead of driving left out of the gate towards the village we turned right and we were in countryside with no proper roads. It was still dark. Dad had to show his ID to a man in a shed who let us go into a bit of land where animals are allowed to be wild. Dad kept calling it the Bush even though there were no bushes. The ground was really bumpy and everyone was bouncing up and down in their seats. It was getting light but the sky was all grey and it felt like a different country from the sunny one where we play on the tyre swing and have to go indoors to stay cool. We watched a herd of antelopes through our binoculars. Stripy marks, pointy horns. Dad said we were using trees for markers, like proper Africans. There was a big tree next to two small ones and Dad said Remember we came past them so we can find our way back. It made me think of that fairy story when the boy and the girl get lost because the birds eat all the breadcrumbs and the thought of getting lost out in the nowhere like that made my heart beat loud. In the story the dad deliberately takes the boy and girl into the forest to kill them because there isn't enough food. I had the thought that Dad was taking us where wild animals were on purpose to kill us like in the story and once I thought it I couldn't get rid of it. I knew it was a stupid thought for me to have, the kind Robin would hate, and I knew it wasn't real, but nothing was real so it didn't make any difference. I didn't want to think that thought so I shut my eyes.

There was no sound apart from Dad talking. He started telling us some of the adventures you and him had before we were born, like when you stayed in a hotel with a rat in your room and one time when you slept in the desert with no tents and there was a gun battle going on in the distance. Robin said he wanted to have an adventure and Dad said We're having an adventure now, aren't we? Robin said Home is boring you just get to go to school and that's it. Dad said Sometimes life gets in the way and because my eyes were shut I could hear his voice go sad but then it changed when he said Let's carry on driving and maybe we'll see lions.

We drove and drove until Zami tapped Dad on the shoulder which meant Stop. He pointed and Dad used his binoculars. That was where the kill was. The kill was a dead buffalo with its guts all on the ground and a lion was there, lying a little bit away. It looked like a shadow. Dad was really pleased, shaking Zami's hand

and saying Well done, man, well done. He asked Zami if it was Young Lady, like Zami was the expert, and Zami said I think so. There is one lioness who wants to be a member of the big lion gang but the others won't let her. All the safari guides call her Young Lady. The other lions are a family and they don't like the one on her own. No one knows where she came from or why she's always on her own. Dad said maybe her mother got shot or attacked by hyenas which have got the strongest jaws of any animal. He said to me and Robin Imagine how impressed your friends will be when you tell them you've seen lions in the wild. He was really excited and so was Robin. Zami was just normal and I was trying not to think about Dad driving away and leaving us for lions to attack.

Daylight was coming and the sky looked like someone was colouring it in, as if a giant hand was choosing red for the sun and pink for all around it. Purple for the hills. I was in a picture of Africa with Dad and Robin and Zami but you weren't in it.

We stayed for ages while the day began. The others were waiting for Young Lady to eat the dead buffalo and I was waiting for Dad to make us get out of the Jeep then drive away and leave us. I was twisting and twisting my scarf but luckily Robin couldn't see because he was sitting in the front.

The lioness just stayed under the tree. I had a go with the binoculars but they made everything jiggly and all I could see was my own eyelashes. Tell us more adventures you had with Mum, I said. I was trying not to think about that fairy story. Dad said we needed to be quiet otherwise Young Lady would never move or do anything but after ages of sitting there with no one saying anything and the lion just looking at us he said that when you and him came home you had the biggest adventure of all. Robin said What was that? Dad said Having you guys, of course. Robin said That doesn't sound like much of an adventure but Dad said no matter how many amazing sights you and him saw before and how many places you visited, me and Robin were your biggest adventure. He went all serious about how we were the best thing that ever happened to you and him and he asked if we still had the photo of the Funny Man. Robin didn't know what he was talking about but I did. It was a picture of you two at a temple with an Indian priest. Funny Man is what we used to call him when we were little because he had a massive beard and face paint. The photo used to be in the hallway in our old house but now it's in my bedroom at Nan and Grandad's.

If you love us so much how come you live in a different country, I said, but Robin told me to shut up and that was when Dad decided to move the Jeep. Sometimes the engine won't start without a whack so he had to get out. I was scared Young Lady would attack him. Don't be an idiot, Robin said, she's got a great big buffalo right there, she's not hungry, but Robin doesn't know everything and she could have been annoyed with us for spying on her. I watched her the whole time Dad was standing in front of the Jeep, waiting for her to pounce on him and rip his head off with her claws, but she just watched him like a lazy Young Lady or like a normal cat that people have in their houses as pets. When he got the engine started we drove right up close to the buffalo's dead body. We could see where the guts had been eaten. Its skin was black but inside was all bloody and red. I felt sorry for it.

Being in Africa is like being on a different planet, not just a different country. Even though I know you came to Africa with Dad before we were born, this time where we are now is a planet where you have never been. It's like when it's rainy at school compared with when it's sunny – they are two separate places even though everything is the same: I am the same, school is the same and the teachers are the same.

We found our way back and the way I made sure to remember the journey was to think of me and Robin for the two small trees we passed and Dad was the big one. There was no tree for you. Even though it was dark and cold like winter when we were having breakfast the sun was burning hot by the time we got back to Dad's house. My legs were stuck to the seat of the Jeep so when I stood up it felt like my skin was being torn off like the buffalo's.

Me and Robin played on the tyre swing. I said to him Don't you think it's strange there aren't any photos of Mum at Dad's new house? Robin said There aren't any photos of anyone, it's not his style. It's true – Dad's house looks like one in an advert with not much in it except sofas and ginormous bowls and vases. Nan's got photos all over the place, including ones of you and Dad and including our really bad school ones like the one from Year Two where Robin's got a mullet. She puts flowers in vases but Dad's are empty or just have twigs in.

We wanted Zami to come on the tyre with us because it's better if two people push but he couldn't join in because he had jobs to do. The sun was high in the sky so we went indoors to get away from it. Robin and Dad were looking through the telescope. I said to Dad Is Zami your servant but Dad laughed and said he didn't have servants so I said What about Silumko and Robin said Silumko is a chef, stupid. Dad said in Africa some people call Zami a houseboy but instead of that he is a friend. I said Zami couldn't be Dad's friend because he's a boy. It seemed more like he was his son. Dad said he already had a son and he put his arm around Robin when he said it. I could tell Robin was embarrassed. Then Dad went into the kitchen bit of the room which isn't a separate room like in most houses. You'll meet another friend of mine this evening, he said. She's coming over later. He opened the door of the fridge when he said it so his head was hiding inside. Me and Robin looked at each other then quickly looked away. Robin pretended to be busy looking through the telescope but I could tell he wasn't seeing anything.

Dad got us some ham and some cheese and some bread for our lunch and we ate it on the shady patio table. I said Why doesn't Zami eat dinners with us and where does he eat them? Dad said Zami eats with Silumko. I asked if Zami's parents were dead and Dad said yes. Then I said something stupid. I said Like mine. Dad gave me a funny look and Robin made a face. Dad said I'm not dead am I and then I said something even more stupid. I said You might as well be because we never see you. Robin told me to shut up and Dad told him it was okay and leave me alone. He started talking in the horrible quiet voice that grown-ups use when they are telling you something bad. He asked if we knew what a Looked After child was and Robin said Yes it means someone who is adopted. Adopted or in care, yes, Dad said. A child whose parents are dead or not able to care for them. Dad told us about the organisation he has made for children with no parents to look after them. Dad and Silumko both help do the looking-after. They have organised a football match for orphans where a cow might be killed to bring them good luck. Who's going to kill the cow? Robin said, and Dad said most likely Silumko or maybe he would kill a chicken instead. It would be killed in front of everyone with everyone watching. When I said that was mean, Dad said it was important to respect different people's beliefs and Robin said there wasn't any difference from an English butcher killing a cow. A butcher is killing for meat, though, not football, I said, and I pretended

I felt sick because of the idea of it. Robin called me a pussy so I ran inside the house. I didn't feel sick but it's true I couldn't stop thinking about the cow.

The other thing I was thinking about was Dad's friend that he said was coming over later. I knew it would be a grown-up woman.

I waited in my room for Dad to come. The next picture in the aeroplane book was a boring one of a truck. I made the road that the truck was on brown first then red over the top but the dead buffalo and all its spilled guts kept getting into my head and so did the football match when Silumko would give Dad a ginormous knife and make him cut the cow's throat. Its blood would gush out and he would drink a big cup of it with the whole crowd watching. In my thinking the cup was a big golden vase like the World Cup and Dad was drinking the blood and it was dripping down from his mouth like a vampire. My picture of the truck on the road grew dark brown and red and bloody. I coloured it in so hard the crayon broke and made a hole in the paper.

After a long time Dad knocked on my door. He tried to talk about Super Mario but what he really wanted to say was that Zami came from a different country, not South Africa but nearby, where he was starving and people were mean to him. Dad's plan was for him to help with holiday guests and train as a wildlife guide. He said tourists and rich people like us have money that can help people like Zami and he understood I might be jealous of Zami but it was important to be kind in the world. What he didn't know was that all the time he was talking the only thing I was thinking about was who his friend was. At the end of his talk I said What's her name and without asking who he said Her name is Beautiful.

KAREN SAT ON THE LOW perimeter wall. She watched Ian emerge from the other side of the temple. When he saw her he came to join her, sitting beside her without saying anything, taking her hand in his. The landscape was bathed in soft pink mist that rose up from the valley. There was no breeze to stir the flags strung across the temple courtyard and everything was still, as if the world was waiting for something to happen, someone to act. A flock of small birds flew past. His hand felt cool. The sun had only just risen. There was no sound apart from an occasional camera shutter.

This was possibly the most beautiful place they had visited but, while other tourists murmured quietly or took photographs or reached out to one another in companionable silence, she remained unmoved. The air was too indeterminate, the delicate colour of the sky was too pale, it couldn't touch her. Instead of appreciating the higgledy-piggledy quality of the dwellings nestling among the hills, she could only think how smug and destructive humans were. She wondered if other people around her were feeling the same, and the idea that they might not caused a kind of vertigo. What was wrong with her? In an involuntary spasm, she gripped Ian's fingers more tightly. He returned her squeeze.

'Let's get married,' he said, turning to face her. He was panting slightly, excited as a boy. 'Marry me and let's have some babies.'

She couldn't speak. Her uncertainty hung in the mist. It seeped up from the ground with the morning dew, and when she looked down she saw that the toes of her walking boots were sodden.

'What do you think? You and me, a couple of kids, some land…' He was still looking at her with his keen boy face.

'Land?' she said

'Maybe even some animals,' he said. 'A veranda where we can sit out and smoke.'

'Will we smoke?'

'If we want.'

She wanted to tell him about the feelings she had that she suspected weren't the same as other people's, as his, but she couldn't find the words.

'A tree with a hammock,' she said instead. There was one in the garden of the hostel where they were staying.

'Definitely.'

'We'll have a girl and a boy,' he said, 'and a dog and a pig.'

'A pig?' she asked.

'Yes, to feed our scraps to.'

A sadhu approached, tapping the ground with a wooden staff. His beard was as white as his robes and his face and arms were chalked white. He gestured at the camera hanging around Ian's neck.

'To take photos of your lovely temple,' Ian said, 'and this moment – so we can remember it.'

The man wagged his finger in a triangle whose points included himself, Ian and Karen.

'A photo? Of the three of us?'

The man nodded and indicated that Ian should ask one of the other tourists to take the picture. Ian approached a young guy, told him that he and his girlfriend had just got engaged and asked if he would mind taking their photograph. The young guy congratulated them and took Ian's camera. The old man adjusted his robes in readiness. The photograph was taken and the old man, having been paid the coin he requested, shuffled away to pose with other tourists.

This was a moment in which the two of them could shed their old selves and prepare for a life of togetherness, Karen thought. It would be a life in which each of them would know everything about the other and a life in which there was nothing that could not be said, nothing held back. Once more a sensation rose up in her throat, shaping itself into words that wouldn't come.

'Who's to say that what anyone sees is the same as what anyone else sees?' she said at last. Even though she hesitated to open up the possibility of difference between them, and to hint at the sense she had of her own difference, this was a safer place than where other words might have taken her.

'Eh?'

'Views like this – or a work of art, say, that people think is brilliant or beautiful… It seems incredible that so many people from different places, different cultures and different experiences can all agree that it's wonderful.'

'I know what you mean,' he said.

'Who's to say it is wonderful?'

By way of an answer, Ian waved his hand at the landscape in front of them and at the ornate temple behind them.

'Yes, but remember the story of the emperor's new clothes,' she said.

'You don't think this is beautiful?' he asked. He looked concerned.

'I do think it's beautiful – I do!' she said, and the importance of what she was trying to communicate made her speech stall, its mechanism unfit for purpose. 'I worry… sometimes… that what I think of as the colour blue, say, might not be what you understand… by the word blue. We might be talking about two different things.'

'How would we ever know?'

'That frightens me.'

'Are you saying you don't want to get married?' he asked.

'No!'

A silence fell between them.

'It's a leap of faith,' he said, after a while. 'Sharing a thought or a feeling with another human being.'

He put his arms around her and they huddled close against the morning chill.

'All this... beauty – it's almost too much,' she said, but her voice was muffled against his body and he didn't hear what she said.

'What?' he asked, but she didn't repeat her words.

'Are you hungry?' she asked, and, taking a last look at the view, they agreed to go in search of breakfast.

'What colour would you call that?' he asked, pointing at the streaked sky. The hills in the distance looked purple.

'I don't know,' she said. 'Indigo, maybe?'

They began their descent down the uneven path cut into the mountainside, watching carefully where they placed their feet because it was so knotted with roots.

I SAID HOW COME your name is Beautiful and she said It is the name my mother and father gave to me. She spoke in the same old-fashioned way as Zami and she moved slowly, like she was in a dream. She was wearing flat shoes like the plaited ones in the wardrobe, except these ones were blue not gold, and she had a necklace with big beads on it. The beads were as big as tomatoes. I wanted to know what if her parents didn't think she was beautiful, would they have given her a different name, but Robin was really quiet and not saying anything so I was too.

I brought the aeroplane colouring book outside to the table where we were having a barbecue and I offered her to help me colour in the next picture, which was a necklace. We were doing the beads in different colours. Dad was pleased. He smiled at her and she smiled back. I said to her Could you write By Indigo and Beautiful at the top please and she did. I wanted to see if it was the same writing as the names on the presents. It was. The 'e's and the 'l's and the 't's were the same.

Robin came indoors and found me looking at the presents. He said he had to get away from the lovebirds. He asked me why was I bum-licking them. Then he saw I was holding a present and he snatched it off me while I was trying to read the names on the labels so I smacked him. Sorry but I couldn't help it. Dad heard us fighting and came in to tell us off. If you had been there you would have made me go to my room but you weren't so I didn't. Because Beautiful was there Dad was showing off by telling us an African saying about sharing the head of a locust. He thought we wanted to open a present so he said Why not and we were allowed to open one each. Open this one, Indigo, he said, and Robin, you open this one. Robin got the headphones he's been going on about. They're red and he looks really stupid when he wears them, which is all the time. I got an iPad. Even Robin was impressed. It was for all of us, Dad said, so we can Skype him from our bedrooms, not from downstairs in the living room when Nan's watching TV. I made Dad open his present from me. He liked the aftershave me and Nan got him. He let Beautiful smell it. I said Sorry, Beautiful, I didn't get you a present. She said Don't worry about it.

Even unwrapping presents didn't make it feel Christmassy. Dad said it was because it wasn't Christmas Day yet but that wasn't the reason. To make it feel like Christmas we played cards and then we played the memory game. I chose the objects. I got the bottle opener with the tribesman head from the kitchen, a pine cone from the dish in the living room, the lid off the sun cream, a yellow crayon and my scarf. I made Dad take off his shark-tooth necklace and we had that too. That's a pretty scarf, Beautiful said, when I laid everything out. I told her it was yours and you were dead and Beautiful said she was sorry to hear that. I said Why do people say they're sorry, it's not their fault is it and Dad said there was no need to be rude, man. I said there was no need to say man at the end of every sentence and Dad said just because it was nearly Christmas and we were on holiday it didn't mean I couldn't get sent to my room.

I'm too good at the memory game. I guessed what was missing every time. I asked if Beautiful was staying the night and Dad wouldn't say yes or no. He said she was spending the evening with us. When it got late I sat in between them on the sofa so they couldn't cuddle. We watched a film about a man who wants to kill himself but an angel comes down and saves him. It was really boring. Robin watched it with his headphones on. When it finished he was yawning so Dad said Time for bed, buddy and Robin went. Then it was just me. What about you, treasure, Dad said, but I wasn't tired. Even though the lemon mosquito candles were making me have a headache I carried on watching telly. Soon Beautiful said she was going to bed and she stood up and walked really slowly. Everything she does, she does slowly. I couldn't imagine her running to catch a bus. She stepped up the big steps from the sofas slowly and then, instead of going through the doorway with the antelope skull over it where our bedrooms are, she went the other way, to go out to the roundhouse. She looked as if she was gliding. She said Night, Indigo and I said Night-night back but I never took my eyes off the TV.

I must have fallen asleep because then I was in my bed but wearing all my clothes. The sheet was over me and the mosquito net was tucked in. I could hear Jack's chain dragging as he moved about in his kennel. I took my Alarm Girl when I went to do a wee. Dad's bedroom door was closed so I pushed it ever so gently and quietly. If Dad thought I was a robber he would stun me with his stun gun. There were two heads on the pillow just like I knew there would be. One was Beautiful's. I thought about pulling the pin out of my Alarm Girl. If I did, the screaming would wake them up with a fright. I stood and I stood with my hand on the pin and their heads on the pillow but then I went back to my room.

I was wide awake so I finished colouring in the necklace picture. I made all the beads red. Even though I was thirsty I knew if I had a drink I would regret it.

THEY CAUGHT THE TRAIN SOUTH especially to make their announcement. Karen wondered if her parents had guessed their news.

'We've got something to tell you,' she said after they had ordered their meals.

There was a prickle of tension in their corner of the pub restaurant and Ian's foot found hers under the table. She rushed to say the words she had planned, but she was so nervous that only an unintelligible burst of sound came out.

Ian laughed. 'What your daughter's trying to tell you is that I have asked her to marry me,' he said, smiling.

He leaned across the table to address her father.

'I would have asked, Doug,' he said, 'but we were a long way away and I wanted to go with the moment, if you know what I mean? I hope you don't mind?'

'I can't think of a nicer bloke to have as a son-in-law,' her father said.

'Me neither,' said her mother.

Proposing a toast, they held up their drinks and sunlight coming through the pub window glittered in the glasses.

'So did he get down on one knee, Karen?' her mother asked. 'Did you, Ian?'

'It was quite romantic, wasn't it?' Ian said, turning to her. She felt her face stretch into a smile that didn't quite belong to her. 'We read in the guidebook that sunrise was the best time to see the view from this temple,' he said.

'The dawn of your married life, Kaz,' her father said, and her mother told him he was a poet. Karen didn't recognise this sentimentality of theirs. It was disconcerting. Perhaps they were relieved that, by marrying her, Ian was taking her off their hands.

She scraped her chair noisily away from the table.

The chill of the ladies' toilet revived her. She was grateful to her parents and this was an occasion – perhaps the only occasion – to let them know. She loved them, and she would tell them so. She would tell them how being away from them had made her appreciate them. She stood in front of the mirror and silently rehearsed explaining how travelling the world had opened her eyes to the importance of what they offered. What she had thought of as staid and oppressive was a kind of anchor. Her reflection gazed back at her. Why was it, then, that she felt so loose in the world?

'Where's the ring?' her father asked as she returned to her seat. 'Ian says you bought a ring.'

She held out her hand to show them the plaited silver ring and matching bangle they had chosen in Kathmandu.

'Silver not gold?' her mother asked, and Karen reminded her that she preferred silver.

'And now you're getting married that'll be an end to all this travelling, will it, Ian?' her father asked.

'Never!' Ian replied.

Her mother turned to her. 'Oh, but Karen, if you want to make a home, start a family...'

Ian rubbed his hands together in cartoonish glee. 'We'll have babies on the road,' he said. 'One in every country we visit. Dual passports and different citizenship for each child.'

'He's joking, Mum,' Karen said, seeing her mother wince.

'You wait,' her father said. 'Once you have children you'll feel differently.'

'I don't think so, Doug,' Ian replied.

'But some of these countries can be dangerous, can't they?' her mother said.

'Anywhere can be dangerous, Mum.'

'I know that. Do you think I don't know that? I watch the news! My point is, you might have been willing to take a risk in the past but if you have children you have to think about who would look after them if, God forbid, anything happened.'

'That's what godparents are for, no?' Ian said. 'That and forswearing the devil.'

He grinned at Karen but she sensed his strain, could hear the effort in his voice as he grew serious for her mother's benefit. 'No, you're right, of course we'd name legal guardians and all that, but we're not even married yet, let alone pregnant!'

There was a brief pause. Here was her opportunity. Now was the time to thank them for their years of effort: cold mornings when her father helped her with her paper round, lifts and loans he had given her, meals her mother had cooked, skirts and shirts she had sewn, the unconditional love they had both offered. Now was the time to tell them how sorry she was for any difficulty she had caused them – to apologise for the anguish; the feel of the towelling bathroom mat; the sound of her father screaming.

'You and Dad would do it for us, though, wouldn't you?' she said. 'If we did want to name someone? In case something did happen?'

Her mother looked at her and they held each other's gaze. 'Of course we would,' her mother said.

Now was the time to say it. But the peculiar mixture of fear and prohibition in her mother's face meant the words wouldn't come.

After the meal, when Ian left the table, her mother said, 'He's a good person, Karen; you're lucky to have found someone like him.'

'And him,' her father said. 'He's lucky too.'

'Of course, Douglas, I'm not saying he's not. Don't go putting words into my mouth.'

There was a silence between them. With Ian gone, even for a short time, the atmosphere changed.

'Treading on eggshells,' her mother said. 'That's how I feel, anyway. Always afraid I'll say the wrong thing.'

'There's no "wrong thing", Mum.'

'I'm just saying how it feels. I can never tell. I would have thought you'd be happy – '

'I am happy – ' Karen tried to tell her, but her mother continued speaking.

' – and that this would be a happy occasion. For any other family it would be a happy occasion.'

She busied herself gathering up her coat and bag and, when Ian returned, all four made their way to the pub car park where they hovered, gravel crunching under their feet. Pleasantries were exchanged about what a nice meal it had been and how glad everyone was. Then they separated, the couples walking in opposite directions towards their parked cars with the sun dipping behind the buildings.

I WOKE UP WET even though I didn't drink anything in the night. I could hear voices so I knew Dad was awake. I chucked my sheets and pyjamas out of the window and Jack started barking. I feel sorry for him because he's got big fur and he's always trying to get in the shade. That must be why he's so bad-tempered. If I go near him Dad tells me off because he's a guard dog not a pet and he might bite me.

Dad and Beautiful were sitting at the breakfast bar. They were being all friendly and normal because they didn't know I saw them asleep in Dad's bed in the night with their two heads on the pillow and Dad's arms around her.

Robin downloaded a drawing game on my iPad. You can play it online with random strangers. I drew a comb and Eleanor O guessed it. Then I guessed her bucket. Soon I was earning coins for more colours and I was good enough to play on Medium level.

Robin said Eleanor O was probably a man really who was living with his mother and was a psycho. Dad gave us a boring talk about internet safety like they're always going on about at school.

In the afternoon we drove out to a town to buy me some new sandals. Beautiful sat in the front and I could see her face in the side mirror for the whole journey. When she looked at me I didn't look away and nor did she so it was just our two eyes looking and looking and looking at each other. There were kids selling cigarette lighters and oranges at the traffic lights but we didn't buy any. They knocked on the car windows but Dad didn't open them. I didn't want to get where we were going but we did get there. We parked at a beach where there were loads of colourful beach huts like crayons in a box – red, green, yellow. I said When we get back I'm going to tell Zami to paint his shed a bright colour. Dad didn't say anything. I couldn't be bothered to get out of the car and I was being slow so Robin shouted at me.

He told me to stop being such a drama queen. Dad told him to leave me alone, I was just tired, that's all. He said being on holiday was a tiring business. It's true I wished we were back at Nan and Grandad's but with Dad there too and no Beautiful. When we walked along I went in between so they couldn't hold hands.

Dad bought Robin a woven bracelet and some shoes made out of old car tyres. Robin said the shoes were really comfortable. They looked ugly. One of the shops had ballet pumps like Beth's but with little spotty bows on the front. When I wanted some for school Nan said they weren't suitable, even though everyone wears them. Dad didn't know what shoe size I was so I had to try lots on until some fitted. They had clothes too and Dad bought Robin a Nelson Mandela T-shirt and I got a dress with a heart cut-out back. The pattern of the material is of tiny elephants that fade from one colour to another, from green to yellow to orange to red to pink. Sometimes I think Robin is right and I am a spoilt brat. We never used to get so much stuff. Beth says it's because Dad feels guilty but guilty about what? Nan says Ignore her, she's just jealous but I want to know.

We were going to a restaurant and I said Is Beautiful coming? Beautiful said I don't have to come if you don't want me to, it's up to you, so I said No thank you and she said That's fine. Robin gave me a dig but she whispered to Dad it was fine and it was.

Night comes so quickly in Africa it was dark by the time we went there. There were flaming torches on either side of the doorway and waiters in white jackets who carried trays on their shoulders. We looked at the menus and there was every type of meat. There was even crocodile and ostrich to eat. I wanted a burger and for some reason that made Dad laugh. You always know what you want, don't you, Indy, he said and he scruffled my hair like I was a little kid. Robin said he wanted to try something he had never tried before so Dad ordered him something called a Platter. I could tell Robin secretly wanted a burger. Dad said Knowing what you want is a good life skill and he told a story about my first day at school which was that you and him both walked me together on the first day but when we got there I wouldn't let go of Dad's hand. It wasn't what you expected because I knew the school from seeing Robin there and I wasn't shy like some kids. Dad said I wouldn't get in the queue for my new class and the teacher came and tried to make me but I still wouldn't go. You and him had to take me to a corner of the playground and talk about how exciting it all was. And do you remember what you said to us, Indy? Dad said. I didn't. Do you know what she said, Robbo? Robin was pretending to be interested but I could tell he wished it was a story about him instead of me. Dad said I was looking at all the other kids in the playground and he could see that I suddenly understood something because I looked at them and I asked him Does everyone think they're the main one?

Dad laughed and laughed but me and Robin didn't know what was so funny. It was because I was only four when I said that, Dad said, and it was the first time I looked outside myself. I didn't know what he was talking about. He was kind of laughing and crying at the same time. He had to wipe his eyes. He said I was a confident girl who was growing into a confident young woman. Sometimes I don't feel all that confident but I didn't tell him that. And I'm not a woman because I haven't got my periods yet. Obviously I didn't say that either because that's not what to talk about at the dinner table. Then it was Robin's turn. Dad said he was going to be a successful young man and asked if he had lots of friends and if teachers liked him. You're quite a success, am I right, Robbo? At school? Robin said I guess but Dad told him off for being modest. He was talking in quite a loud voice. I think he was a bit drunk. Don't be so modest, man! Your friends, Indigo, they like him, right? Girls, I mean? All the girls in my year say he is fat and what a dork but I told Dad Yes, girls like him and Dad said That's what I thought. Then our dinners came and my burger had a little South African flag on a stick poking through it that Dad said I should keep as a souvenir. Robin said crocodile meat tasted just the same as chicken.

I said It's surprising really, when you consider. Consider what, pumpkin? Dad said. He was all smiley and a bit drunk. Robin gave me a look but I didn't let that stop me. I said It's quite surprising that me and Robin are okay when you consider that our mum's dead. It is, pumpkin patch, Dad said, and he stopped talking loudly and just nodded his head, saying It is, and I thought again about what it is that Beth says he is so guilty about.

HER PARENTS WERE EXPECTED but she was still in bed. She drifted in and out of a queasy kind of sleep, listening to Ian and Robin downstairs. When she opened her eyes Ian was standing in the bedroom doorway.

'Still sleeping?' he said. 'They'll be here soon.'

She closed her eyes and he came further into the room.

'Karen.'

He moved about, picking clothes up from the floor and folding them, opening and shutting drawers. She kept her eyes closed and soon became aware of a smaller, silent force. Ian murmured something and there was a shuffling close by.

'Sleeping, yes,' Ian said. His voice was gentle. He rarely spoke to her in such a voice any more. 'Mummy asleep.'

A salty smell. Warm breath. A child's whisper. 'Ssshh.'

'That's right, ssshh. Good boy.'

Soft movement and then silence.

'Karen. Your mum and dad are here. Get up.'

The bedclothes were pulled back.

'This isn't funny any more,' he said. 'Are you ill or what?'

When she opened her eyes his face was pushed right up close to hers, a giant looking in through a window at a doll.

'Do you feel sick?' he said. 'I brought a bucket.'

The red plastic bucket they used for washing the car. On the floor next to the bed, a towel spread underneath it. The towel had an image of a leaping dolphin on it. She pretended to retch. He snatched the bucket and held it under her chin. She hung over it, hiding behind her hair.

'Don't worry,' he said, patting the bedclothes.

She pulled the duvet over her head, heard him go downstairs. A little while later her mother came into the room. 'This morning sickness, then,' she said, 'it's more like morning, noon and night sickness, eh?'

Karen didn't reply. Her mother sat down on the bed.

'How many weeks are you now? Coming up for fourteen, something like that? You're meant to be blooming!'

There was a silence. Karen didn't move.

'I had it bad, too. Couldn't keep anything down for the first few weeks – they were quite worried, thought they might have to take me in – but it passed eventually. You'll feel better soon.'

Her resistance to all of them – to Ian and her mother and even Robin – gave her a perverse kind of strength. Once her mother had left the room she pushed off the bedclothes and slipped her feet into a pair of old suede moccasins. She put on a cotton dress over her pyjamas and a cardigan over the dress. In the bathroom she splashed water on her face and drew a comb through her hair. She checked her reflection in the bedroom mirror. She looked like someone else.

With one hand on her belly and the other pawing the walls, she moved down the stairs like a blind person, like a person weak with hunger or dying of thirst. In the hallway outside the living room, framed photographs hung on the wall: holiday images, wedding pictures and photos of Robin when he was newly born all testified to a togetherness she had shared. Now she felt remote.

Her father was on his hands and knees building a Lego city on the carpet. Robin leaned against his grandfather with one arm hooked casually around his neck. Ian and her mother directed operations from the sofa.

The door handle felt as if it might melt under her touch. She had a vision of it dripping to the floor and then the door itself cracked and splintered, breaking into sawdust. The Lego city seemed about to dissolve into a pool of molten plastic that threatened to fill the room. It would ooze through the door and move inexorably through the rest of the downstairs rooms, carrying Robin and her father and Ian and her mother in its glutinous mass. The walls of the house bulged, threatening to explode. Everything was about to dissolve or combust.

'Here she is!' Her father noticed her in the doorway. 'Feeling any better, love?'

On seeing her, Robin left his grandfather's side and came over to take her by the hand. Her father stood up, rubbing his knees. She could tell that Ian was embarrassed by her dishevelment as he explained how on top of her morning sickness they had all been a bit below par lately. He hoped her parents wouldn't catch the cold they had all been suffering with.

'That's the trouble with little ones, isn't it?' her mother said. 'What with them spending all day on the floor and so on, they pick up all the germs going. If you want me to have a go at your skirting boards, Karen, I've got a pair of rubber gloves in the car.'

'You're our guest, Val,' Ian said. 'You don't need to bring your cleaning equipment!'

'That's what I told her,' Karen's father said, 'but would she listen?'

Even though she recognised their words, Karen could make little sense of them and she had no words of her own to bring to the conversation. It was as if they were speaking a foreign language that she understood only in part. She hadn't mastered the spoken version. She felt her parents' eyes on her, darting away from hers if she caught them looking, but watching her all the time, taking turns to follow her, listening closely to the few words she said – as if trying to crack her code.

It was only Robin that she could understand with any confidence. The savoury smell of him and his biscuity breath – none of this required translation. She concentrated on the warmth of his small hand in hers and got down on her knees to be next to him. Before Robin, she hadn't known it was possible to feel such connection – not to anything, not even to herself. With his soft voice in her ear as he talked her through the cityscape laid out before her on the carpet, she felt herself return to the world of others. Light from the living room window sharpened their features and she began to see them more clearly now. She felt like Sleeping Beauty, awoken with a kiss, returning to the normal, waking world.

'Sorry if I was tough on you earlier,' Ian said, once her parents had gone and Robin was in bed. 'It's no picnic being pregnant and your parents can be hard work.'

'It's okay,' she said. 'It was fine, wasn't it? In the end, I mean. Robin had a nice time.'

'You're not feeling so sick now?' he asked, watching as she wiped a piece of crusty bread around the casserole dish, mopping up its remnants.

She heard the need in his voice, registered the baffled look on his face. She nodded. What he didn't know was that she recognised the dullness that hung like a mist all around. Mostly, she could pick her way through it. With Robin as her guide and the green and red and yellow of his Lego pieces like Hansel and Gretel's breadcrumbs, she was able to find her way. Sometimes, though, it descended so thickly it was impenetrable. Everything was cloaked and she too was cloaked and veiled in a mist of her own, that might lift at any moment or might remain in place, obscuring her from the world and removing the world from her. She had never found words sufficient to explain this veiledness to him, never when she was under it and not even at times like now when she was more free of it. Perhaps it was better for him not to know.

I WOKE UP THINKING the worst because I drank two Cokes at the restaurant but I was dry. I put on my elephant pattern dress to celebrate. Today was what Dad called a Chilling Day. He was on the phone loads so he said we could just hang out. I was glad. It reminded me of when he lived in England and he was at work and you would say Today is a Pyjama Day. I asked him if Beautiful was coming round but he said she was working. He said it in his annoying gentle voice. I said What is her job and he said she was a seller of houses. I wanted to know if she sold Dad his house but I didn't ask.

I was getting really good at the drawing game. I kept guessing Eleanor O and CatladyUK's pictures. I thought Picasso might be you because I could guess Picasso's drawings straight away and Picasso could guess mine. We never didn't guess and the drawing of a baby was exactly how you would draw one – all chubby with a wiggly line on top of its head for its hair. I thought maybe you weren't dead and instead you were living somewhere with a new family and new children playing the drawing game with me while they were at school and not having Pyjama Days. Maybe you found a new boyfriend and had a baby and Dad thought we would be so sad to find out that he told us you had died instead and had a fake funeral and sent us to live with Nan and Grandad.

Another possibility was if Dad wanted to live in South Africa and be girlfriend and boyfriend with Beautiful maybe you weren't living with a new family. Maybe Dad killed you. People get money when another person dies. Maybe that's why Dad is so rich. When I look at him I am wondering if he could do it and how he did it if he did it. On the news in England there was a man who killed his wife by driving her car into a river. If I think about the car sinking and the water coming in if you open the windows I feel like I'm drowning and my legs and arms start swimming even though I'm on dry land.

Zami said he would take us into the village if we wanted. Robin said Are we allowed? I went indoors to ask Dad but he was on the phone. I heard him say The kids don't know yet and I wanted to know what we didn't know so I hid in the corridor to our bedrooms and I heard him talk about an airport pick-up. He didn't know I was listening but the front door was open and Tonyhog came tip-tapping in so Dad got up to shoo him out and saw me. He laughed and said What are you doing lurking around here, Indy? I thought you were outside. I could tell he was nervous that I would find something out.

I went back outside and I told Robin that Dad said we could go to the village even though I didn't ask. We walked along with Zami like he was our proper friend and like we lived in Africa instead of being on holiday. He taught us some of his language and when people said hello we said hello back and when they asked us how we were we said we were cosy. Zami was going to see his sister on a bus and I wanted to see her too so that meant Robin had to come. I bought us all Cokes with my own money and I told him Dad said we could, which served him right.

The bus journey took ages and there were no seats free so we had to stand up. When the bus went around corners we fell over. It was hot and bumpy and the driver played loud music. Some of the people on the bus talked to Zami and even though they were speaking a different language I could tell they were talking about Robin and me. Robin didn't like it. He wasn't saying anything to anyone. Why aren't you speaking to me, I said, but he wouldn't answer. We got off the bus in a marketplace. People were carrying shopping on their heads but they stopped what they were doing when we walked past. There were lots of dogs, but the kind you don't touch in case they've got rabies. The buildings were sheds made out of tin. Robin said we should be getting back now but we had only just arrived and me and Zami wanted to say hello to his sister. Zami said we would be quite quick. I whispered Africa Time to Robin, which is when nothing is quick, but he ignored me and took my scarf off me so he could hold it up against his nose to stop the smells coming in. The smells were of burning cooking and rotting rubbish.

We came to a battered old door with its number painted on the front. The woman who opened the door was Zami's sister. She had a pink towel tied around on the outside of her clothes. Her house was really dark. Robin didn't want us to go in but Zami made us by waving his hand and saying please and frowning when Robin said we wouldn't. A toddler was on the floor and there was a bed in one corner and some shelves with nothing on them. The floor was red and the walls were blue. The toddler liked the bows on my new shoes and if I moved my feet he tried to get them. Zami was talking to his sister in their language and I was playing with the toddler but Robin was just standing there holding my scarf over his face even though there were no smells inside Zami's sister's house. I tried to get him to give my scarf back but he wouldn't. Zami's sister had a serious face and she didn't speak to us, only to Zami in a foreign language, but when she saw the toddler playing she laughed and her laughing voice was different, just like Zami's. When he's with Dad he doesn't laugh but when he is with me and Robin he does sometimes laugh and it is a different sound from his normal voice, as if he's got two different voices, one for speaking and one for laughing.

I noticed there was a tiny baby wrapped up in the towel that Zami's sister was wearing over her clothes.

It was having a piggyback but it was fast asleep. It was a boy, Zami said, and thank goodness he was healthy. When Zami's mum died him and his sister had to live with his grandmother. Same with me and Robin, I said – but the difference is that Zami's grandma got too old to look after him and there wasn't enough food so first his sister came to South Africa and then him. The last words their mother said were to his sister and what she said was Look after Zamikhaya. It was our mother's dying wish for us to stay together, Zami said. His sister's name is Nomsa and Zami said her husband was a bad man. At first he helped them and said he could get jobs for them but after the baby was born he wanted Zami's sister to go and live far away. In Africa the baby belongs with the father's family. Zami's sister wanted to stay with Zami so she ran away from the husband and now she was all alone. The toddler who liked my shoes wasn't her baby, she was looking after it for somebody else and they would give her food in return. I said to Zami Why don't you bring your sister and her baby to live at Dad's? Not the toddler but the tiny sleeping baby in the towel. I said I would ask Dad but Zami didn't want me to. I said Why not, he wouldn't mind but Zami said Your father has done enough for my family already. When he says father he says it like this – fatha.

Robin wanted to go, even though we had only been there a short time. There was a bus waiting at the market. This time it wasn't so crowded. I said to Zami It's so sad about your granny and your mum and your sister. Robin gave me a dig and said Don't get involved. The whole journey I kept thinking about Zami's mother's dying wish. I was thinking what your dying wish was. Robin doesn't look after me. He doesn't do anything with me except be mean. When I asked for my scarf back he threw it at me and said Have your stupid baby scarf.

I was trying to remember what were the last words I heard that came out of your mouth. I think it was Night-night.

When we arrived back at the village near Dad's all the little children were holding our hands and laughing. They ran away when we got to our gate. Zami stayed behind to talk to Lindisizwe and Dad came storming out of the house looking really angry and wearing smart trousers. He shouted because he had been looking all over for us and he didn't know where we were. I told him we went into the village and he said we were only allowed out of the gate with him. It felt like we were his prisoners. I said Why are you wearing that outfit and he said I haven't finished with you, young lady, but it will have to wait because there's a surprise for both of you indoors.

Whenever anyone says that, I think the surprise is going to be you. We went indoors and there, sitting on the sofas, were Nan and Grandad. It wasn't you. Robin said What the – ? and his face was like in a cartoon when the character looks and then looks again and their eyes go ginormous because they can't hardly believe what they are seeing. Dad said Now we can all be together as a family for Christmas. It was Christmas in three days' time but it didn't feel like it and Nan and Grandad didn't feel like Nan and Grandad because they looked different in Africa. Grandad was all shy and Nan's hair was all big and standing up where she'd back-combed it like she does when she wants to give it body. It was weird them being there – as if it wasn't really and truly them. Dad tried to put his arm round me but I didn't let him. He said Sorry I got so angry, Indy, but you have to understand there are different rules here. Neither of you had your phones with you and I didn't know where you were.

Nan said she couldn't believe the place Dad had and wasn't the garden lovely. She was wearing a yellow T-shirt I had never seen before. It had a big white bird on it and the sleeves had white beads hanging off. You never get to see her arms normally, but in the summer you do and they're all freckly. It was summer here even though it was Christmas. That's a colourful top you're wearing, Nan, I said, and she said to Dad She doesn't miss a thing which is what she always says about me. How about that dress of yours, that's new, she said, and she noticed Robin's new T-shirt too but she didn't say anything about my shoes so I knew we would have an argument about wearing them to school. She bought her bird T-shirt at the airport when they were waiting for a lift. Dad said Sorry about the wait and Robin said Africa Time and everyone laughed. Nan said Don't I get a kiss then and me and Robin had to kiss her and

Grandad. Then we all went and sat on the big sofas. Dad said Both of them are doing so well, meaning us, and Grandad said we were lovely kids. I know that, Dad said, but you're doing a good job is all I'm saying and I want to thank you. No need, said Grandad, and he wouldn't look at Dad. They were all talking as if they didn't know each other and none of us were looking at each other. I was looking at my shoes which were all dusty from the village and I couldn't wait to clean them. Dad was talking about all the things we were going to do while Nan and Grandad were here, like safari and posh restaurants. We were going to an island with a prison on it the next day. Nan said it was very generous of Dad to pay for their holiday and he said they were welcome any time and it wouldn't cost a penny.

There is a narrow white line running around his neck, where his necklace goes. If you lift up his necklace you can see what colour he would be if he lived in England not in South Africa. It would be the line to cut along if someone was chopping his head off.

WIND RATTLED THE WINDOW frames and whistled through the thin walls of the rented cottage. Karen could feel its draught as she stood at the main bedroom window watching trees bend. In the moments when it paused she could hear Ian talking with the children in the room next door.

'When adults get fed up or tired they don't cry like kids cry, do they?' he was saying.

'Why not?' Robin asked.

She heard Ian hesitate and the wind, too, held its breath, like a child crying, gathering energy for the next wail. 'Because they're grown-up, I suppose,' he said. 'It's the kids' job to cry, but the grown-ups have to soldier on.'

'Soldier?' Indy's voice now. It cut Karen to the core.

'Sometimes Mum feels like being quiet, doesn't she?' Ian explained. 'Sometimes we all do. And we just have to leave her be.'

She moved quickly away from the bedroom window and went downstairs. There was a sensation of being followed and she knew what the feeling was. She knew not to look back over her shoulder.

Rain spattered on the coals. It was ridiculous to light a fire in summer but the cottage was freezing. This holiday was a disaster. Several times they had bundled the children into waterproofs hoping to walk to a nearby beach, but each time the weather had turned them back. Today they had spent the day indoors trying to play board games, but at four years old Indigo was too young for most of them, so Ian had made her a shop underneath the table where her merchandise, comprised of their own belongings and random items from around the cottage, remained on display. They had put the kids to bed early – it was still light – and now the evening stretched out ahead of them.

'Robin wants you to go up,' he said, coming into the room. There was a glass of wine in his hand but he hadn't poured one for her. She was afraid he was reaching the limits of his tolerance. He had been earnest and patient in his bid to understand why it was that she could become rigid – petrified, almost – but soon he would demand that she account for her behaviour. She had a vision of him with an enormous ledger in which he would list his complaints and ask her to explain herself.

There were no answers she could provide. The sums wouldn't tally.

'It's not helping,' he said. 'The way you're being.'

Rain whipped the windows. Time slowed. When he spoke, his voice sounded unnaturally loud, and yet she knew he was speaking normally.

'The kids are feeling it and so am I,' he said. 'What's going on?'

With his question came the rushing sensation she had been dreading. With his words it gathered momentum, like an urgent beast that had collapsed in pursuit of her, and now staggered to its feet. It thundered towards her with frightening speed. Its weight was immense, this bull in the china shop of her mind. If she didn't talk about it or address it by name she could keep it at bay, but if she made eye contact she would be done for. If she acknowledged it, it would come for her, like an animal from the wild that, once allowed into the home, would ingratiate itself perhaps, and appear tame, but nonetheless retain an awesome and frightening power that it could unleash without warning.

She held Ian's gaze, willing him to sense the energy in the room.

'Robin wants you to go up,' he said once more, and a great gust buffeted the house. Something fell from the roof and clattered to the ground outside the back door. Ian sighed and turned away from her.

She climbed the narrow staircase and found her children motionless in their beds.

'I don't like this house,' Robin said.

His limbs were in outline under old-fashioned sheets and blankets. The room smelt of mildew and a dream-catcher hung limply from the lampshade, its tendrils thick with dust. She and Ian had visited so many other places – stunning places, full of colour and noise and heat; how had they had ended up in a damp holiday cottage where dreams become clogged in deposits made up of strangers' skin cells?

The wind shrieked and she was afraid the flimsy walls might crack and topple, afraid she herself would crack and topple. She imagined plaster and bricks tumbling around them, burying her and the children. The weight of the debris compressing her head from all sides would be a relief, balancing out the heaviness inside her mind.

Or perhaps the ferocious wind would catch the cottage and fling it into the sky. A powerful funnel would whisk all four of them into a vortex, swallowing them whole. Or else it might explode, the owners of the cottage having planted a bomb timed to go off at precisely this moment, combusting outwards, windows smashing, bright splinters of glass piercing her from all sides, slicing her skin and spiking her eyes, gashing the palms of her hands, stabbing her. The bedroom came back into focus. Her skull tightened; imagined wounds throbbed. The eiderdown on Robin's bed was one of the old-fashioned kind, its shiny, silken material cool under her fingertips. Its barely-thereness was intolerable. She knew what she must do. What she must do was go downstairs and drop a glass on the stone floor of the kitchen, lacerate herself. It would release her, if just for a while.

She stood up quickly from the bed, heard what must be her voice say goodnight.

'Why do we have to live here?' Robin asked.

'We don't live here,' she replied, speaking slowly, as if to a foreigner, or as if she was the foreigner.

'Are we going back to our old house?'

'Of course.' She made her way to the door. 'This is a holiday, isn't it? We're just staying here for a little bit.'

'Why?' Indy's voice came from the other bed.

'Why?' She hesitated. Glass shards waited for her. 'To see what it's like.'

She switched off the light. Her children were two humps in the dimness of the strange room.

'To see if we like it?' Indy asked.

'Yes.'

There was another shape in the room too, indistinct in the gloom but vivid in its malignancy.

'I don't like it,' Robin said.

Her mood was infectious. She was infecting them all with it. She mustn't wait for the house to explode or a storm destroy it or a tornado carry them all off into blissful oblivion; better for her to leave now, or when it grew dark. She could walk across the headland to the edge of the cliff, throw herself on the rocks.

'Dad says if the weather's better tomorrow we can go to a beach where there's lots of sand,' she said. The words were so thick in her mouth she had trouble moving her tongue around them.

'I don't like sand,' Indigo said.

'We'll be going home soon,' she said, trying hard to make her voice sound like it should.

She went back downstairs.

'How were they?' Ian asked, coming into the kitchen.

'Okay.'

'Christ knows, I'm trying,' he said.

She stared at a glass she held in her hand, willing it to fall from her fingers.

'I get nothing from you,' he said.

Her fingers remained tensed. She couldn't seem to loosen them. The glass remained whole. She couldn't even summon up the will to break something.

'You know what,' he shouted before he managed to control his voice, 'if you don't feel like talking or being part of this family, just let me know.'

He reached for the cardboard sign he'd made for Indy's shop. It hung on the back of one of the dining chairs and had the word *Closed* written on one side, *Open* on the other. He yanked it off the chair and looped it around her neck with *Closed* facing outwards. 'Closed for business, right? Let me know when you're open.'

His earnestness was gone, and his handsomeness, too. His voice was loud and his short hair made him look like a thug. He left the room and she remained, feeling like a dunce, in the corner. She had to keep still, because of the brute that was coming for her. If she kept still, the bully might not see her.

'It's not new,' she said.

'What's not new?'

He was in front of her but they were no longer in the kitchen. She didn't know what had happened to the glass that was in her hand. She didn't know what had happened to the kitchen.

'The feeling inside comes further out,' she said.

'I don't know what you're talking about,' he said. 'You're just annoying me now.'

She wanted to tell him about a time before she knew him, but the words were too frightening and would summon the beast, which was what she was trying to avoid.

'I just want to be a normal family,' he said, breathing hard.

She had no idea how long they had been sitting on the sofa. She looked past him, checking the room for clues. The fire had burned low in the grate. His wine glass was empty. She could hear him trying to regulate the amount of air he was taking into his lungs.

'Let's give up,' he said. 'Let's go back.'

She let out a little moan.

'What's keeping us here? We don't have to stay. Karen!'

He gripped her tightly by the wrists and shook her. She allowed herself to be shaken. She wanted him to shake her, in the hope that he might be able to shake her out of herself.

WE WENT ON A FERRY to the island where Nelson Mandela was a prisoner. In the car on the way Nan and Grandad and Dad were all talking about his funeral. Grandad said people might start rioting and Nan said they didn't riot when he was alive because he suffered enough. She said even though she didn't like Nelson Mandela's tactics when he was a terrorist it was dreadful to be locked up for so long. Dad didn't agree that he was a terrorist and Nan said We'll agree to disagree then, shall we, Ian? That shut him up. If she calls him by his name like that he goes quiet.

Robin couldn't believe we were going to the actual prison where we could stand inside Nelson Mandela's real prison cell. Lots of other people were going too and it was in the middle of the sea. Everyone felt sick on the ferry because of the waves and the engine smoke.

Grandad tied my scarf around my face like a cowboy which was good because all I could smell was their house and no one could see my face, only my two eyes. Robin puked in a bag.

When we got to the prison a man gave us a talk. He told us before it was a prison the island was for lepers, and I noticed Nan kept rubbing her hands with handwash after that.

The man giving us the talk used to be an actual prisoner. Everyone was interested apart from me. I wanted to go on the iPad but Dad said it would be inappropriate. Inappropriate is a word that teachers say. They could say something is bad or wrong but instead they always say it's inappropriate. It's annoying. Nan asked the man was it true about Nelson Mandela knitting to stop himself getting bored and the man said yes it was true and he was the father of our nation. I wished I had some knitting to do.

Everyone apart from me was sick again on the ferry back. I was the odd man out. Nan said I was like an ox. When we got back Dad asked us for some business advice. He showed us the website he is designing for his company. Nan said I was too big to sit on Dad's lap but I stayed where I was. Dad's website has photos of his house and the beehive cottage and loads of countryside and animal pictures and one of Dad playing golf. It says Taylored Travel – Travel With You In Mind on the homepage and there is some writing about how South Africa is a safe and exciting place for family holidays.

Nan asked if it really was safe and Dad said It's perfectly safe, Valerie. He called her by her name and she said to him You know Doug and I are more than happy to hang on to the kids, Ian, calling him by his name too. Dad said It's perfectly safe. Then Nan said But there are no memories for them in South Africa and Dad said Maybe that's a good thing.

We were all staring at a page on Dad's website that said This Blog Is Still Being Built Please Come Back Later and Dad said we could do with a fresh start. Then I said to Nan Have you met Dad's new girlfriend? Of course Nan said no. Her name's Beautiful, I said, and Nan thought I meant she had a beautiful name so I had to tell her that her actual name was Beautiful. She got confused but in the end she said That's an unusual name and I said Yes because what if you were called that and you were really ugly? Dad said he could introduce Beautiful to Nan and Grandad and Nan said that was entirely up to him. He tipped me off his lap after that and I could tell he wished I didn't mention Beautiful to Nan.

Later when I was in my room Nan came in and asked me loads of questions. She said it was only natural Dad would want someone special in his life. Everyone needs someone, she said. I was feeling a bit sick. I don't feel like me, I said, and Nan thought it was because of the ferry but that wasn't right because when everyone else was being sick Grandad said I was like a sailor with sea-legs.

I was afraid it was malaria not seasickness and Nan could read my mind because she asked if I had taken my medicine. When I told her that Dad took my pills away because they would make me go weird Nan said what would I prefer, going weird or dying of malaria? She said I was too precious to take a chance so I should carry on taking the medicine. I said What about Robin and Nan said he was precious too. She said she would speak with Dad and she would make sure everyone kept taking their medicine.

SHE WENT TO SEE her doctor. She wasn't well. The doctor gave her a prescription and she collected it from the pharmacy while Indigo stood patiently by her side, as patiently as she waited now, for her mother to fetch down paper and crayons from a shelf that was too high for her. The vulnerability in the slope of her shoulders as she stood waiting, her gaze fixed on the shelves in front of her, and the round of her buttocks in red corduroy trousers that were a size too small and hoisted too high, slayed Karen. She had to look away. There was a tightness in the room, like the increasing pressure of a migraine attack. Holding on to the edge of the kitchen counter while the whole room slanted away, she moved to the sink, steadying herself on furniture like Robin and Indy had when they were learning to walk.

She held a glass under the tap. The rush of water was deafening. She placed the glass carefully on the table, barely disturbing the surface tension of the water.

Its transparency was a relief – its nothingness and its purity – but, as she stared, the glass and the rim of the water's surface became an aggravation, its surfaces and boundaries defining too much the end of something and a beginning of something else. She yearned for an absence of lines or shapes or elements or objects. A blankness, like the white of a page for drawing, like the white of a smooth oval tablet.

Tired of waiting, the little girl came over and took her mother's hand. Karen felt the transfer of droplets from the glass of water between their fingertips.

'Wait a minute,' she said, and she gulped from the glass, tipping back her head to swallow the tablet.

Together they moved to where the drawing things were and Karen fetched them down. Soon her daughter was bent over paper, the ends of her hair skimming the page.

The phone rang and the earlier tightness crept into the room once more. Karen listened to herself have a conversation with her husband. There was a thickness in her throat, as if she might vomit or weep. Their talk soon dwindled into nothing, matching the sensation she had of herself. If only she had something of the vigour of her child, who clutched two crayons in one hand, dragging a red trail and a blue trail across the page and on to the table top.

'I can't talk,' she told Ian. 'I've got nothing worth saying.'

Indy lay down her crayons. She picked up the piece of paper and turned it around for her mother to see, holding the page in front of her own face. 'Guess.'

Karen stared at the swirl of red and blue, two loops either side of a triangle and a circle, two long spidery lines. It was a figure of some sort. Even though the images were basic, mostly she was able to guess them accurately. She couldn't tell if her rate of success pleased her daughter or if she would prefer her to get it wrong sometimes. She cleared her throat before speaking.

'Lady?'

'A Mummy with wings,' Indy said, and, replacing the page on the table top, she took up two crayons in one fist again and began hailing down a shower of red and blue bullets. Karen reached out a hand to stroke her head but Indy shook her off so instead she combed through the collection of pens and crayons, finding comfort in the simple task of putting on lids and testing colours. Making a pile of ones to throw away gave her a sense of purpose, although she knew even as she separated them that she would be incapable of disposing of them and would end up putting them back with the others.

At the doctor's surgery she had listed her symptoms and the doctor had tapped out a rhythm on his computer keyboard. Now, sitting at the kitchen table, the thud of her daughter's crayon on the paper seemed to echo the doctor's beat, as if both daughter and doctor were trying to tell her something. She closed her eyes against the stark white of the page, against the white of smooth oval tablets in their packet, one dissolving in her bloodstream now. She tried to decipher the communication, concentrating on the punctures of sound emitted by each stab of the blue and red: two colours clenched in the fat little fist.

'Why have you got your eyes closed?'

There was no pause in the thudding rhythm for the question but, when Karen didn't answer, the noise stopped.

'Why are your eyes shut? Are you making a wish?'

Karen nodded, trying to relax her mouth, trying to un-frown her brow. Then, the tap-tap-tapping of the doctor's computer keyboard started up again, his typing re-patterned in the stab of red and blue, blue and red, pressed tight together, thumping over and over on the page, making a blizzard of tiny marks.

'A wish, yes.'

She opened her eyes. The room billowed and pulsed. The walls throbbed, as if she and Indigo were inside the beating heart or bowels of a beast. She gripped the table edge.

'Did it come true?'

Karen opened her mouth to answer but her tongue was stuck, as if she hadn't uttered a word for a hundred years.

'Did it come true?' came the question again.

'I don't know yet,' she said.

ON CHRISTMAS EVE I stayed in my room all morning. Everyone was annoying me. Nan was being annoying,

Dad was being annoying and of course Robin was annoying. In my room all the folded-up things in my case were annoying so I scribbled and scrabbled them up and threw them all about so there were clothes on the bed, on the floor, everywhere.

In the yard the sun was beating down even though it was Christmas. There was no sign of Zami or Tonyhog and there was no sound, just the buzzing that Robin says is insects taking over the world. The chickens were hiding from the heat under Dad's car. I opened my shutters and held on to the bars at my window, seeing what it would feel like to be Nelson Mandela in prison.

I was thinking about you and Dad and whether you were really in love. The way Dad and Nan are is a clue. Say Dad didn't love you and he wanted you and me and Robin all to die so he could be with Beautiful, a good way of doing it would be to kill you and make me and Robin catch malaria. There would be no evidence.

Eleanor O drew a desert island and I guessed it. She guessed my kitchen and CatladyUK got computer. When I got Picasso's birthday cake there was a message. It said 'What colour is Indigo?' Robin would say don't answer because it could be a paedophile but I knew it was you because you guessed my birthday cake in two seconds when I drew a Little Mermaid one like the one I had when I was eight.

Dad said Wow, what a mess! when he saw all my stuff on the floor. Why don't you come and have some lunch, puppy doll? I didn't go and I didn't go and at last

Nan came to find me. She said We're going to a posh hotel for tea, I think your Dad's trying to impress us. I tried to think what his plan was and if he could sneak poison into the food. I knew I was being stupid and that kind of thing only happens in stories but it didn't stop me thinking it.

Dad said it would be nice to wear a dress or a skirt to the hotel. I wore shorts instead. Everyone was waiting for Beautiful. Nan was giving me looks and checking I had sun cream on even though I knew all that because I had been here longer than her. She always fusses over me but not Robin. She says it's because I'm a girl and girls are a worry but that's sexist.

I was with Tony when Beautiful came. He lets me scratch his back now, and I can pull him quite roughly by the tusks like Zami does. His eyes are brown, like mine and yours, and just like a human's. Robin doesn't believe it but he understands everything we say, even more than a dog. When he heard Beautiful's car he ran around to the front of the house to say hello. I hid behind the Jeep where the chickens go. She didn't even look at Tony. She walked straight past him. She was wearing an orange dress with a thin belt. She had flat orange shoes to match, and white bracelets on both wrists. The white showed up against her skin. Dad came out of the house and kissed her. I got in the Jeep and picked more stuffing out of the torn seats. Soon there will be none left and the seat will be just metal. It will be too uncomfortable for Dad's clients to sit on.

Robin came out and called my name but I ducked down and he didn't see me. I picked and picked the seat stuffing. Zami came around shushing with his broom like he does every day even though there's nothing to sweep. Tony went with him. Then Silumko came out and him and Zami sat on the back step eating porridge. They ate it with their hands instead of with spoons and they ate it in silence. I tried to make the sound of the bird I always hear but they knew it was me not a bird. I whistled at them and they looked but they couldn't see me. In the end Tony showed Zami where I was. It was a good game and I wanted to play it again but Robin came out and said it was time to go. While the grown-ups were getting ready Zami taught us how to drive the Jeep by showing what pedals to press and how to change gears.

I didn't want to go in Beautiful's car and Robin didn't either, even though it was an Audi. We made Nan and Grandad go with her and we went with Dad. It was a long journey. I watched Dad's driving the whole time but he didn't do it like Zami did. He put it on to Automatic Pilot and it drove itself. Beautiful's car was in front and I could see Nan and Grandad's heads like they were little children. I knew Nan would be talking in the posh voice she uses in shops and on the telephone. I thought about who would die if we had a crash. Beautiful and Dad could have a sign and suddenly smash their cars into each other but duck down at the last moment so they didn't go through the windscreen. They would live happily ever after.

We did a walk at a place where there were colourful birds and monkeys so tame you could touch them, even though Nan said not to. It wasn't a proper safari, though, it was more like a zoo. The monkeys were scratching in the dust and making patterns. Beautiful said they were looking for insects to eat but it seemed like they were trying to draw. One of them drew a line that looked like a path going up a mountain. It looked like he was doing a drawing of where he lived. Beautiful was pretending to be a safari guide even though she works in an office. She kept getting me and Robin to stand with Dad and have our photo taken. Grandad was sweating. Dad asked if he was alright and Nan said did he want to stop and have a sit-down but Grandad said he was fine and would everyone stop treating him like he was ninety-nine instead of sixty-nine.

We went to have a look at where Beautiful works. The people in her office shook our hands. Her name was on the desk and a sword was on the wall. She let Robin hold the sword. It was a Zulu sword even though Beautiful isn't a Zulu. She's from another tribe. Beautiful's tribe are famous for their dancing. She said tourists like Zulu swords and Nan said They like dancing too – one day you must show us your dancing. Robin asked if the sword had killed anyone but Beautiful said it was just for ceremony. She should have told him it killed someone, it would have made him like her. Grandad was sucking up by asking all about history and Beautiful was just talking to him all the time, no one else. Whenever Nan said anything she was talking in her posh voice and Dad was smiling the whole time and pretending we were a normal family. Me and Robin were the only normal ones.

We went to a big hotel with a café in the garden. Dad was totally bum-licking Nan because he knows she loves that kind of thing and he was trying to get her to like Africa. Nan said the tea was delicious and the cakes were delicious. Everything was delicious. Dad and Grandad talked about politics. Me and Robin just sat there being bored. Robin wasn't allowed to wear his headphones. The hotel was famous in the olden days for apartheid and when I didn't want anything to eat or drink Dad said was I doing it as an anti-apartheid protest and Robin got all annoyed. She's not being political, he said, but Dad kept saying I was on a protest. I had a fizzy kind of headache that Nan said was my hormones but Dad said it was because I hadn't eaten anything. Then him and Nan had an argument about malaria. Dad told Nan she had given us the wrong medicine and I said would he prefer me to go mad or die from malaria. Robin got angry. He called me a drama queen and said he was sick of all of us and stormed off through all the tables in the garden with all the people watching so in the end Dad didn't get to show off and Beautiful knew for sure we weren't a normal happy family.

When we got back, Zami was outside the gate talking to Lindisizwe and another man who was so skinny he looked like a drawing of a stick man and who was wearing a woolly hat even though it was sunny. We ate stew that Silumko made and Nan asked Beautiful to show us her dancing. Beautiful said she didn't have the proper skirt and she only dances at weddings. Grandad said he would like to see her traditional dancing and because he said it she couldn't say no. Dad said he would be her drummer. It was embarrassing. Dad was drumming on the table with his hands and Nan was clapping, but totally in the wrong rhythm. Beautiful was standing on the grass and stamping her feet a little bit and turning around in a circle. It wasn't actual dancing.

Afterwards, Beautiful walked around the garden with Grandad showing him all the plants and telling him about them, like it was her garden not Dad's. Grandad's head only reached up to her shoulder. She called him brother instead of his name and when I said to Dad he's not her brother why's she calling Grandad brother he told me the word she was saying was bava which means father. He's not her father either, I said, and Dad started going on about African customs and boring stuff like we learn at school. I yawned on purpose.

I used to yawn when I was doing my homework. You used to tell me off but I couldn't help it. Even though homework is boring I wouldn't mind doing it if you were sitting next to me like you used to.

I went to find Zami. The crickets were loud and the moon was lighting up the sky. I had my torch and my alarm. I stood on tiptoe to look through the window of his shed and I could see him reading. His house was all concrete. The floor was bare concrete and the walls were too. There were no pillows on the bed and his chair was two blue crates on top of one another.

When I knocked on his window and he saw it was me, he marked the page like Nan does, by folding over its corner in a triangle. The book was one of Robin's animal guides. I said Is this what you do at night and he said Read and write, yes, it is important. He is making a whole book the same as Robin's but in his own writing because books are expensive. I said You can have my DS if you want, I don't play it much any more but he didn't say thank you even though he is so polite and even though that was kind of me and a DS is more expensive than a book.

I told him I wanted to go and see the Young Lady lioness and he said it was best to see the animals at night when they are hunting. It's night now, I said. You could take me. He said I would have to ask your father. I told him about Beautiful's dance and about her pretending to be a safari guide but he didn't say anything.

A moth kept batting itself against the lightbulb. His torch was on the desk. I shone it right in his eyes. Neither of us knew Morse code so we made up our own. One flash for yes, two flashes for no. If you like the idea, shine it once, I said. Zami picked up the torch and shone it on the wall. Then he clicked it off again.

Jack started barking and we heard Dad telling him off. He was coming to find me. I could tell he was angry because of the way he said my name. He told me off for not having long sleeves on when it was mosquito time. You wouldn't even care if I caught malaria, I said and he said Don't be silly, it's time for bed. Then he told Zami there was a hole in the fence to mend the next day. He put his hand on the back of my neck and steered me out of the door. On the way back to the house he shouted at Jack for barking. I went to bed without saying goodnight to anyone apart from Zami, who I said it to by shining my torch at his window.

In South Africa people go to the beach on Christmas Day and have a barbecue. None of us wanted to go to the beach because it was too hot so Dad said we could stay at the house instead. We opened our presents from under the tree and Nan and Grandad brought presents from England. Mine was a black and white skirt with polka dots on and a letter from Beth that made me homesick.

No one was playing the drawing game because they were too busy having Christmas. I waited ages for Picasso to guess my crossword puzzle and it came with another message. It said Well done and I knew that was your way of saying Happy Christmas. It wasn't a happy day though.

I wore my new polka-dot skirt with my new ballet pumps that were all nice and skiddy on the tiled floor. Robin asked me why I was dressed all fancypants and when I told him to shut up he said Alright, no need to get arsey. Nan said Language, Robin, but Dad didn't tell him off. He just said to ignore Robin because he doesn't know anything about fashion. Nan said my skirt looked nice but when I looked down at my new shoes the black leather made my feet look really pale and big. They looked like two shiny black cars sitting next to one another at the traffic lights. The sun was all glary and the smell of the barbecue coming in through the windows was making me feel sick. I wasn't feeling like me and it wasn't feeling like Christmas.

You used to wear your smartest clothes on Christmas Day and so did Nan but because it was African Christmas she was wearing shorts. You could see all the veins in her legs. Blue for blood with no oxygen in it.

I thought the barbecue was going to be sausages but it was a whole baby pig with a metal spike through its body that turned it around and around over the charcoal until it was cooked. Its eyes were closed and you could see its eyelashes, all crispy and burnt. It had little hairs on its tail like Tony. I didn't want Tony to see it. If he came round to where we were sitting I would shoo him away. Luckily he didn't come. I think he stayed away because he could smell it.

No one ate much, not even Robin. Nan said No one likes eating a big meal when it's hot, not even if it's Christmas Day. She said it in her polite voice mixed with her gentle voice that she normally uses for saying hello to Minnie over the fence.

Grandad said the heat was too much for him and he was going to have a lie-down. When he was gone Dad said I made a mistake, didn't I, we should be having roast turkey in England like normal. Robin said No, it's good to try different things, which is what Nan and Dad always say to him.

Nan started watching one of the old films Dad gave her for Christmas. I think she was doing it out of kindness because his cooking was a failure and Christmas was a failure. Dad went in his room and shut the door but I listened outside and I could hear him talking on the phone. I think it was to Beautiful. He was telling her how nobody ate the barbecue.

I spied on Grandad when he was asleep in the little round cottage. He was lying in a star shape on the bed with his mouth open. I did a cough but he didn't wake up so I made another noise with my foot but he still didn't wake up. When I got nearer I could smell his smell of medicine and of old cheese. I could smell the thatched roof too. His things were on the table next to his bed – his wallet and heart pills and malaria pills. I picked up the malaria pills and shook them. He did a great big sigh that made me jump but he didn't open his eyes. The name on the bottle was Douglas Arthur Forrester. In his wallet there was a photo of you. It didn't look like you, though, or maybe I forgot what you looked like. On Nan's side there was a book with a lady on the cover. She looked mysterious because her hat was covering her eyes. Nan's make-up bag was there. She's only got old make-up but her lipstick is okay. I put some on and I sneakily put some on Grandad but not on his lips. On his cheek. A dot, like on a doll's cheek. He did a big snore. There was a glass of water with bubbles in it where the water was old. Mosquitoes like old water so you shouldn't leave it standing around like that. I poured a little bit on Grandad's bed near his feet. Then I poured a bit on his knees. Then I dipped my fingers in and sprinkled the water so it was like rain coming down on his face. That woke him up. He was a bit shocked. He sat up in bed really quickly and said What the devil – ? When he found out it was only me he panted like he had just been running and said I was lucky he didn't have a heart attack. He asked what I thought of this place and I said I don't know, what do you think of it? He said he didn't think much of what he'd seen so far. I said You're going to like the football match tonight though because we were going to watch the orphans play. I told him there was going to be a sacrifice and I said What do you prefer, England or Africa and he said England, much, even though your Dad's lawn puts mine to shame.

Dad's present to Zami was a Manchester City football shirt that he got Grandad to bring over from England. I couldn't find the water container to make Tonyhog a mudbath so I knocked on his door to ask him where it was. When I said Happy Christmas Zami said Happy Christmas To You. A bit like people normally say Happy Birthday To You. What's it like when both of your parents are dead, I said, and he said Not good and he looked at me and I looked at him for a long time with nobody saying anything. Tony needs water, I said, and

Zami came with me. We had to pour loads and loads because as soon as we poured any the earth drank it all up and it disappeared – you would never know it had been there. After his bath Tony lay down in the shade all stretched out on his tummy with his back legs out behind like he was a human. I wondered if he missed his bushpig friends but Zami said once a pack of wild bushpigs came near the edge of the garden and Tonyhog ran away.

When it was cooler in the day it was time for the football match. We drove there in the car and the Jeep. Silumko drove the Jeep with me and Robin and Zami in it. We waved at people and shouted Happy Christmas.

It was a proper football ground with seats for the audience to sit in but instead of grass for the pitch it was just bare ground. All the players were wearing red T-shirts with Play For Hope written on the front and Taylored Travel on the back. Beautiful was there. She was wearing a red T-shirt too. When Dad kissed her she said What do you smell of and he laughed when he told her it was my Christmas present.

I wasn't looking forward to the sacrifice. Dad said I didn't have to look if I didn't want to. Robin said he was going to look. Nan said the idea that killing a cow or a chicken could bring good luck was a load of rubbish. Dad said Please don't talk about Silumko's beliefs in that way, Valerie.

Zami and the other players did a march around the pitch and Dad did a speech through a loudspeaker.

Silumko was standing next to him and another man was carrying a live chicken under his arm like a handbag. I didn't even see the knife. One minute he was cuddling the chicken and the next minute he was tipping it upside down so its blood could pour out like a jug. He poured it out all around the penalty spot. I couldn't believe I had seen something die right in front of me. I saw that chicken alive and then I saw it dead and the world carried on apart from that one chicken in it. I was sitting down but I thought I would fall over. Nan said I was white like a sheet is white and Grandad made me put my head between my knees but then the football match started and everyone was jumping up and down. Nan said Come with me, Indy, you'll feel better after a little walk.

We followed the line of the football pitch all around its edge and I asked if that was a faint I did when the chicken got its head cut off. Nan said she reckoned it nearly was. I asked if she ever fainted before and she said Never. I could see the others watching the football match in their red T-shirts while me and Nan were separate. She told me about different customs in Africa and all over the world where a man can get his hands chopped off if he steals something and a woman can get acid thrown in her face for driving a car. When Nan talks about different people's customs it's more interesting than it is at school. Her voice goes all quiet and crackly and her body gets close. It was so close my feet were going off the line of the football pitch and into the game.

I had to keep looking at the line to make sure we didn't go over. Nan said there are some places in Africa where people bury real live babies under their new house for good luck. Whose babies are they, I asked, but she didn't know. Anyone who doesn't want them, she said, or who believes in the sacrifice. It's a kind of blessing they believe in. And you thought a chicken was bad enough, she said – that's not the half of it. I was feeling a bit sick and I didn't want to be separate so I made Nan go back. We had walked around the whole football pitch three times and Dad said my face had some colour in it. Robin and Grandad were calling out to the players like they do when they're watching football at home and shouting at the television. It was as if they had forgotten we were in Africa. Robin had Grandad, Dad had Beautiful, and all I had was Nan walking around the edge of the football pitch telling me about dead babies. That was all I had and I didn't want it. It was Christmas Day but I was glad it didn't feel like Christmas because without you nothing is the same. Without you everything is different.

IT WAS A QUIET afternoon. Karen and Indigo were brushing dolls' hair.

'What are we going to do today?' Indigo asked.

'You said you wanted to do dollies, no?' 'Do dollies' was a phrase of Indigo's from when she was young. She was beyond playing with dolls now, Karen suspected, but with the house to themselves 'doing dollies' was what they were doing.

'We could go out if you like,' she suggested.

'Where to?'

'The swings?'

The girl didn't reply and Karen softened with relief. The prospect of getting both of them dressed and leaving the house was exhausting. She pulled a hairbrush through a doll's nylon fibre hair. Sometimes she felt as plastic as the creature in her hands.

'Where's Robin?' Indigo asked.

'He's at football, isn't he?'

'Where's Dad?'

'At work.'

She watched her daughter wrestle a tiny jacket off slender plastic arms. Asking after her brother indicated her unease, which caused a heaviness to press on Karen's chest, as if a great weight rested there. At least the weight was inside now, instead of outside and all around, threatening to invade her and overtake her. Inside, she could accommodate it. She felt a familiar sense of shame – shame that she found normal existence so hard. Ian said everyone found it hard but she didn't believe him. If it was true, why did people choose to live like this? The most trivial elements of existence seemed to require stamina she didn't possess. This was what made her ashamed. She wouldn't live this way given a choice, she often thought to herself, and yet she had the choice. They talked about living in a cave in Spain or a village in Africa but it was only talk. To make it more than a conversation would require strength she couldn't muster. Once more she was confronted with her own lethargy.

Her children were too young to detect her sense of failure. While they were little they had no barometer with which to measure her. They were a sanctuary. Even so, it was a struggle to disguise her feelings from them.

'Want to play the egg game?' she suggested.

'What is it?'

'The egg game – you know. We used to play it when you were little.'

Indigo couldn't remember.

'We wrap ourselves up in duvets,' she said, 'and we wait until we hatch.'

Together, they pulled bedding off Indigo's bed and fetched the duvet from Karen and Ian's bed and made a soft, pulpy mountain in the middle of the room. Disney characters on Indy's duvet smiled contortedly in the hillock's humps and folds. They burrowed underneath, clumping the quilty mass all around them.

'Now we're in our egg,' Karen said, inhaling the musky, biscuity smell of their surroundings.

They sat quietly for a few moments before Indigo asked, 'What happens when we hatch?'

Her voice was low next to Karen's ear and it filled her with such love and longing, she wanted to stay like this forever.

'We have to wait quite a long time,' she whispered.

They remained still and she listened to her child breathing. After a while she wondered if she had fallen asleep. She didn't dare move for fear of disturbing her. She shifted her weight slightly.

'What happens after we hatch?' came the question once more. Karen felt a flush of panic.

'What happens?' Indy persisted.

'We find out what kind of creatures we are,' Karen said, and there was sudden movement as her daughter announced she was hatching into a princess. The duvets were thrown off and daylight from the bedroom window broke up the softness into dazzling shards.

Karen helped to lift the lid of the trunk where dressing-up clothes were kept and watched Indigo hunt for the costume she always chose. She pulled out a silk scarf whose bronze lettering spelled out the word P.A.R.I.S. Karen's father had brought it back from a business trip when she was a girl. She knotted it around her throat.

'Passports, please, ladies and gentlemen!' she cried with the false cheer of an air stewardess.

Hearing herself, she could almost believe her own enthusiasm. She felt like the real thing.

'All aboard flight one two three,' she said, and Indy stared at her with the look of hers that her teachers commented on. Pre-school nursery workers had mentioned it too, even when she was little. It seemed to unnerve people, as it unnerved Karen now.

'All aboard flight one two three,' she repeated, wilting under her child's gaze.

NAN SAID THE BLESSED chickens woke her and Grandad up early with their cockadoodledoing. I said to her did she wish it could have been one of those chickens that was sacrificed but she said Best not to talk about that poor chicken. She said it would be nice for me and Dad to do something together just us two. Dad was going to take me to a famous beach and restaurant. Robin was jealous. I said he could come too but when we got in the car it was only me and Dad.

On the journey, Dad asked me if I was happy at school and how I was doing and if I had a boyfriend and what about maths, did I think I could do with extra help? I said school was fine and I'm okay at maths and all the boys are idiots. What about living with Nan and Grandad, he said, is that working out alright? I miss Mum, I said, and he said That's natural, you're bound to miss her. I told him I missed him too. Why do you have to live in Africa and we live in England, I said, and he just said what he always says, about setting up a new life for all of us. He told me about a school I could go to where it's just girls and you get to wear a dress and a straw hat for the uniform. He said How do you feel about staying in South Africa? I said Forever? He said If you like. What about Robin, I said, and he said Robin would stay too, of course, but he would go to a different school because the one he was telling me about was just for girls. I wanted to tell him about Zami's sister and how they wanted to be a family together but I knew I wasn't allowed so I just told him I didn't want to go to a new school and I didn't want him and Beautiful to be girlfriend and boyfriend. I twisted the corner of my scarf into a point so sharp it hurt when I poked it under my thumbnail. Dad said Robin was right and a big girl like me shouldn't be carrying around a thing like that. It's not a thing, I said, it's Mum's scarf.

The beach was really famous. It wasn't one of the ones where you get Great Whites. On some beaches they blow a loud horn if one comes and everyone has to get out of the water as quick as they can. There was a photoshoot going on, with big lights and models waving bits of cloth around. Their clothes got wet because they were in the waves. Dad was really embarrassing – he went up to one of the make-up people and asked about what they were doing and he asked her if she thought someone as pretty as me could end up as a model. Of course she said yes but only because he asked her, she didn't mean it. Dad said I could do anything I wanted in life. I said I don't think I'm pretty and Dad said Yes you are. He bet me five pounds in English money, not South African, that I would have a boyfriend soon. I said The boys at my school are stupid but Dad told me I was going to start being interested in things like that, it's only natural. Dads can find that kind of thing tough, he said. It's when you need your mum around most of all – to talk about things like boys. We were walking along the beach and I couldn't keep up. The sand kept swallowing my feet and I couldn't hear properly because of the wind. I thought he was going to say he was going to marry Beautiful and she could be our new mum so I told him I didn't need one. We learn about periods and stuff like that at school, I said, and I've got Beth, too. Dad said Beth doesn't necessarily get her facts right.

Some people won't go on holiday to Africa because they think they'll get eaten by lions or Great Whites. They are the kind of people who don't do anything with their lives, Dad said. I said Everyone does something with their life. Dad said lots of people don't make the most of their time living on this planet. Life is short, he said, and time goes really quickly. Time seemed to be going really slowly though, I thought. It felt like we had been on holiday for ages. Beth might not recognise me by the time we go home.

The worst thing is that you never said anything. When Zami's mum died she said goodbye to him and she told his sister to look after him and have a better life.

We sat on the beach on our towels. Dad had the blue one and I had the red one. I wished we had an umbrella but it was too windy for one. Dad said me and Robin could be in some of the photos on his website. He needs pictures of people having fun. We had a joke that Robin would have to hold his tummy in. It's because Dad cares that he wants Robin to lose weight, compared with Nan who lets him eat chips. Dad said Nan and Grandad have a different attitude. He was going on about making the most of everything because you don't know how long you've got and I said Do you think Nan and Grandad make the most of their life? Dad said it was up to them how they live but I could tell he didn't mean it. He said he wished you and him could have come out to South Africa, not just him on his own. I said I wished that too – then he would have you as his girlfriend, not Beautiful. I said to Dad that instead of getting fainter in my mind, you get stronger. Even though it's hard to remember what you were like when you were alive, I can feel you all around like the sky. Dad said Let's go for a swim, Last one in's a sissy.

The waves were big and people were on surfboards. Dad dived straight in. The water smashed into me and I dived in after him. I got my head under straight away. Dad said How's your swimming these days? Be careful not to get out of your depth. The waves were massive. He was shouting and smiling and I was shouting back. Hold on to me, he said, I won't let you go, but his body was too slippery and I was afraid I couldn't touch the bottom. All I could see was turquoise and green sparkles, like the sequins on the mermaid picture on the wall in the old house that I did when I was little. They were getting in my eyes and blinding me. I was trying to tell Dad to go shallower but the waves were too loud and there were little rainbows in my eyes when I looked into the sun. I was trying to hold on with my arms and legs and he was laughing but it felt like he was trying to drown me because I wasn't making the most of everything and because I was mean to Beautiful. Then there was a crash and everything was bright nothingness, then dead. A thump against my chest like an elephant charging. No sound. My ears full of nothing, my mouth sewn up like I didn't have one, my eyes open blind. Deadness. Then a loud rushing noise, like a screeching of brakes and my legs dragged forward, scraping along rough tarmac, burning on the bedroom carpet with Robin pulling me along with my head all wrapped up in my bed sheet, me suffocating and laughing at the same time. I didn't know where I was and then with a whoosh I was upside down.

I was coughing and choking but the water was only shallow. Dad was far away waving and calling, asking if I was alright. I scrabbled back to the shore and Dad came wading back. His hairy chest was all dragged downwards so it looked like animal fur, with his shark-tooth necklace all tangled up in it. The sea is very powerful, he said. It should never be underestimated. It felt like a live thing that was trying to kill me, though, and I couldn't be sure it wasn't him.

After that I didn't want to go in any more. Dad tried to persuade me but he had to go by himself while I watched. The salt was stinging my cheek so I lay down under the blue towel. I tried to get the mermaid sparkles in my eyes again so I could remember the picture. I don't know what happened to it. Dad must have packed it in a box when we went to Nan and Grandad's or maybe he threw it away. It was a good picture. I did it when I was about four or something. Thinking about it made me feel sleepy. The wind was lifting my hair off my face and it reminded me of how you used to stroke my head. If I couldn't get to sleep you would sit on my bed and stroke my hair, remember? On the beach under Dad's towel the wind was still strong but I could barely feel your fingers. I needed it to be stronger for me to remember how it felt and to remember what you looked like sitting on my bed at night.

When we got dressed I found out I had lost my scarf. Dad was asking me why I was hopping up and down but I couldn't help it. My body wouldn't stop moving – even though I tried to make it, it wouldn't obey me. We walked back where we had come from with me half running half falling over in the sand. He asked the make-up lady if she had seen it but it was nowhere. Someone must have picked it up, he said. They could even be wearing it, lucky them, think of it like that. Someone got lucky today, man, like getting a present for nothing. I thought I saw it miles down the beach, crumpled up on the sand, but it was just a rock.

We went to a restaurant even though I wasn't hungry. It was so near the sea the waves smashed against the windows. Dad said it was special glass that could never break. He wanted us to sit at the table at the front but it was booked up so he made the waiter let us sit there by giving him some secret extra money. The waiter put Dad's money in his pocket and we were allowed to sit at the table by the window. My legs were shaky, though, and I felt weak. Every time a wave crashed it made me jump. Dad said Had enough of the sea for one day, puppy and I said Yes.

The waiter lit a candle on our table even though it was daytime. I didn't want anything to eat. I wanted to go home – not to Dad's house or Nan's house – I wanted to go home where you and me and Robin and Dad used to live, even though it didn't have a proper garden but me and Robin had a sandpit. I liked it there. Dad was ordering with the waiter but in my head I was trying to put all the scraps of you together – the sound of your voice when you called out that dinner was ready and the smell of mashed potato that you used to cook that is different from Nan's or from mashed potato in a restaurant. The look of your hands in the sink when you were washing up without your rings on and the look of your face when your hair was wrapped up in a towel after you had a bath. The smell of your clothes when you used to lean over to kiss me night-night. All of them were pieces of you like a drawing that got torn up because it went wrong. I was trying to collect all the little bits back together and remember what the picture was like. Everyone says you were ill for a long time before you died but I never saw you ill.

When I was little, if I was sick you would bring me the washing-up bowl and put a flannel on my head and call me Go-Go.

Thinking about you calling me Go-Go and about someone else wearing your scarf and about me and Robin not looking after each other at different schools and about Dad trying to drown me so I could meet you in Heaven if there is one made me start crying a bit noisily. Dad didn't know what to do. He said to the waiter that we had changed our minds, we weren't eating after all. I wanted to rush out and knock all the tables over but I couldn't move my legs. I was stuck and I was shaking. People were staring and Dad was saying stuff to me but I couldn't really hear him, like when I was under the sea with him trying to drown me with no one looking. Everyone was looking now. A woman with blonde hair who was wearing massive earrings got a blanket from one of the waiters and put it around me. She said I was in shock. Dad told me to take deep breaths and when I did I could smell the earring woman's perfume and I wondered if she could be CatladyUK or Eleanor O or Picasso and if she was I wanted to stay with her forever.

VALERIE SAT IN BED reading. Her skin cleansed and moisturised, according to her nightly ritual, and the day over, she couldn't concentrate on the book in her hands. Doug would be home soon. Partly she welcomed his return after a weekend's separation, but partly she dreaded the possibility of an awkward atmosphere like the one that marked his departure. Some couples thrived on awkwardness. Some women she knew seemed to have some permanent misdemeanour of their husbands' to report. They were always punishing their menfolk for something or other.

Doug wouldn't stand for punishment but he was no stranger to her withdrawal from him. Sometimes he wouldn't know what he had done wrong. Sometimes he hadn't done anything wrong. He put these retreats of hers down to what he called her 'dark days'. Well, he had dark days too.

No sooner had she conjured him in her mind than she heard the slowing of a car's engine and the crunch of tyres on gravel, as if she had summoned him with the power of thought. She tested herself, as if taking her own temperature almost, to see if she was willing to provide an attentive audience for his traveller's tales, but, in the time it took him to fetch his bags out of the boot of the car and walk from the car to the front door, she decided he wasn't deserving of such a performance. She switched off the bedside lamp, the sound of it masked by the simultaneous click of the front door, and when he came into their bedroom she lay still in the dark, facing the wall.

The next morning she was awake early. She made them both a cup of tea, bringing it back to bed as was their custom. Light filtered into the room through the flowered curtains. She arranged her nightgown under the bedcovers and waited for him to sit up and put on his glasses.

'It'll get cold,' she said, after some minutes passed without him stirring. Then, 'How was the trip?'

In a mirror image of the way in which she had presented herself to him the previous night, he remained with his back curved away from her. She could tell he was awake. Karen's alarm clock sounded in the room next door and after a few moments their daughter's footsteps padded across the landing to the bathroom.

'It was a success,' he told her, in answer to her question, but not until much later, when all three of them were seated at the breakfast table.

'Did the others enjoy it?' she asked.

By others she meant Margie Lawrence and the rest of the wives.

'Yes, everyone did. You were missed.'

She shrugged. 'I'm not one for travelling.'

'It was only France, Val.'

'Yeah, it's only France, Mum.' Karen said. 'When I went to Dieppe with the school it only took a few hours.'

'Let's not go into all that again,' she said, sensing them ganging up on her as usual. 'Are you ready?'

Doug got up from the table and went out into the hallway where his salesman's briefcase and Weekender luggage sat neatly under the coat hooks.

'I got something for both of you,' he said, coming back into the room with two plastic bags with *Duty Free* written on. Inside Karen's bag was a clear plastic cylinder containing a doll in French regional costume. The doll wore a full skirt and white blouse with puffed sleeves and a red cape. Her black pinafore apron was decorated with tiny flowers and lace. The nylon fibres of her brown hair shone and her mouth was a dainty rosebud. Her eyes, though, were clumsy dashes of the same black paint that covered her pink plastic feet to represent shoes. The doll looked as if she had been blinded in some violent attack. Or perhaps she had been like it from birth. Catching herself wondering if the disfigurement was an inherited condition, Valerie thought she must be going mad. This Margie Lawrence business had tipped her over the edge.

'Thanks, Dad.' Karen kissed her father. 'I'll call her something French. What's a French name?'

'Françoise,' Doug suggested, and he caught Valerie's eye as he said it.

Karen asked if she was going to open her present too. She reached inside the plastic bag. Her husband had evidently been so taken with Margie Lawrence and her charms, or indeed so occupied with 'Françoise', that he hadn't thought about his wife or daughter until he was passing through Duty Free on the way home. In the bag was a flat cellophane package. She unwrapped it and held up the silk square it contained. It was brown and gold, with the word P.A.R.I.S spelled out in bronze letters over and over.

'Very nice, thank you, Douglas.'

'Some of the other wives bought them,' her husband said, 'so I knew it would be alright.'

'It looks expensive,' she said.

After Karen left, he said he should be making tracks too. Valerie sat at the dining table without clearing the breakfast things. She wondered if the other wives really had bought silk scarf souvenirs. It wasn't the kind of thing she would wear. It wasn't the kind of thing any of the other wives would wear. It was just something else coming into the house for her to find a place for. She folded the scarf. She would put it in Karen's drawer when she went upstairs. The thought of all the things in all the drawers of the house oppressed her.

Margie Lawrence was probably having a lie-in this morning, after yesterday's travel. She would be exhausted after the weekend. She would have got on with the other wives, even the ones she had never met before, and the husbands too. She would have tried out her schoolgirl French in the shops and restaurants and at the hotel she would have laid out all her purchases on the hotel bed for Dave Lawrence to admire before going down to dinner with the others. Dave would have offered to pay for everyone's meal and called the trip a 'team effort'. The others would have raised their glasses in a toast to the company. Doug and Valerie would have raised their glasses too, if she had been there, but, as she had told Doug often enough recently, they weren't that kind of couple.

DAD TOLD NAN AND GRANDAD about the idea of us staying with him in Africa. Nan and Grandad went quiet. It's a big life out here, Doug, Dad was saying, but Grandad didn't say anything back. Everyone crowded around Dad's laptop and we looked at the website of the girls' school Dad told me about. There was a different school for Robin that had a swimming pool with diving boards. Dad had it all planned out. He said he would pay for Nan and Grandad to come and visit us whenever they wanted. Nan asked me and Robin what we thought. Robin said he wanted to go to school in South Africa. He didn't mind if me and him went to different schools. He said our school in England was rubbish because it didn't even have a swimming pool, let alone diving boards. I said What about Beautiful, would she be here too? Dad said we didn't have to decide right now.

Robin didn't believe me that I nearly drowned. I wanted to tell him that maybe Dad did it on purpose but I knew he wouldn't believe that either. He would get annoyed and call me a nutter. We were on the tyre and I told him I lost your scarf at the beach. He said it was a good thing because I looked like a moron fiddling with it the whole time. I said That scarf was the only thing of Mum's I had but he said we had loads of your stuff.

Not here, I said, her scarf was the only thing I brought with me. There's nothing about Mum in Africa, it's all in England. He stopped talking then and I could tell he was thinking about you. He said Let's go and get Zami, it's better when there's three. I said What if Dad marries Beautiful and wants her to be our new mum? Robin said We would just have to suck it up like Beth had to when her mum and dad split up. Beth's mum didn't die though.

Zami was mending a hole in the fence where the jackals got in but he came with us on the tyre. When I told him about nearly drowning he said there was a river nearby where boys jump off a ledge into the water and one got eaten by a crocodile. I imagined the boy jumping straight into the crocodile's open mouth, even though I know it wouldn't happen like that. If I was drawing a picture of it happening I would draw it like that because it would make a better picture than the crocodile twisting the boy around and around and holding him under water until he drowned, which is what really happens. The true version would be more difficult to draw.

No one was talking, we were just taking turns swinging backwards and forwards over the giant hole that's going to be a swimming pool, thinking about what it would feel like to drown and thinking about me and Robin going to different schools instead of the same one.

You better make sure the school Dad gets for you has a good art teacher, Robin said, which showed he was thinking about the same things as me. Then he said maybe the nicest thing he's ever said to me in his whole life. He said I was a better drawrer than Beth and a better drawrer than him (it's true) even though they're both older than me.

Even though he won't let me speak to him at school because he says it's embarrassing, I like it when I catch sight of him in the corridor. Our new schools would be two different schools instead of the same one. Robin's would be the one with diving boards.

The next morning the big living room window was right open so the whole world felt like it was coming into the house. Dad and Robin were doing exercises in their bare chests. Grandad had sweat patches on his shirt even though it wasn't him doing the exercises. He was looking through the telescope. Nan was sitting on the sofa with her handbag, like she was going somewhere. I said Where are you going but she said Nowhere, I'm just taking in the view.

I ate my cereal in my room. Robin came and found me when I was drawing family against CatladyUK and waiting for Picasso to guess my suitcase. I drew a label like the ones me and Robin have got on our suitcases with our names on as a clue for you. We were up to thirty-two non-stop right guesses.

Robin told me to be nice to Beautiful. I said You don't like her either. True, he said, but I'm doing it for Dad. He started doing press-ups in the middle of my room. I don't want him to marry her, I said. Robin put his headphones on but I carried on talking. Maybe Mum wasn't ill, I said, and Robin had to turn his music off to hear me. I said it again – Maybe Mum wasn't ill. He said What are you talking about, you numpty? If Dad was in love with Beautiful and wanted to marry her, I said, maybe it was murder. That made him angry and he stopped doing his press-ups and snatched the iPad off me. He said why were girls so mental and wasn't it about time I stopped thinking about you the whole time. Nan heard us rowing and made him give me my iPad back even though she says I'm addicted to it. She made Robin go and have a shower and wash his mouth out with the soap.

I couldn't believe he would say that. I'm never going to stop thinking about you. I am like a tree and you are the sky all around. There is nothing apart from you and me and maybe a family of lions that comes to lie in the shade of me when the sun gets too hot.

In my room I thought about when it was my birthday when I was going to be nine. I wish I had never opened any of my presents because they were the last ones that you ever wrapped up. I had a daydream that you bought all my presents and wrapped them up but then you found Beautiful's lipstick on Dad's shirt and you tried to attack him with some scissors but he got them off you and stabbed you instead and the police never found out. It was a daydream but it felt like it could be true. What made it feel real was how Nan and Grandad act when they're with Dad. You were their daughter so they wouldn't like to be near someone that murdered you. They have to be nice to him but you can see they're pretending.

I wanted to tell them what I knew but when I found them I couldn't say the words. I asked if we were going out instead. Nan was still sitting on the sofa with her handbag. She said her and Grandad were going with the flow. I couldn't stand to be sitting with them and everyone not saying what they were thinking so I went to find Zami.

He was wearing an old T-shirt with holes in it instead of the new football one Dad gave him which made me think he doesn't support Manchester City or he is a boy who doesn't like football. Or maybe he is saving it for best. I said to him Why don't you wear your new football top? He just sort of smiled without saying anything.

Zami says a child never stops loving its mother because a child chooses its mum out of all the mums in the world so why would we stop loving that special one? Before I was born I must have chosen you so that's why I will always love you and think about you even when you're dead.

IT WOULD BE INDIGO'S birthday soon – they had talked about getting her a bike or a dog, maybe. Wrapping her coat more tightly around her, Karen took Ian's arm and drew herself into his warmth. Her leaning her weight against him caused them to veer momentarily off the path. She looked back over her shoulder to see how far behind Robin was trailing. He was sulking because they had insisted he come on a walk with them instead of allowing him to stay at home on the computer. Every now and then there was a flash of orange plastic bag among the trees where his sister moved about gathering sticks and bark for a school project.

There had been moments in the past when Karen had doubted her capacity for this kind of a life; when she'd doubted that what constituted 'normal' standards of happiness could be hers. Medication helped. The ringing in her ears had stopped and she had a feeling of having reached a kind of plateau. From this height she felt safe. She was able to look out on everything that might have caused her anguish before.

It was possible to be happy. It was possible to walk in the woods with one's sulky pre-teen son and one's daughter hopping about collecting debris in a plastic bag.

'So what if we destroy the planet?' she said, realising too late that Ian hadn't had the benefit of the thoughts leading up to her statement.

'Er, what? Where did that come from?' He was laughing.

Thinking about Indigo's birthday and planning a family get-together now that she was feeling better, she had been thinking about her parents and how different they were from Ian's. They could seem so narrow in their outlook compared with his, who always seemed more cosmopolitan. Ian's parents were separated and living with new partners. They owned second homes and travelled widely. Her own parents lived more modestly. They could appear small-minded and unadventurous but they lived their lives without harming anyone. They were insignificant, in the best possible sense.

'As long as we don't mess things up too badly it hardly matters how we live, does it?' she said. 'Sooner or later something else will come along; someone else will take over. Like when the dinosaurs died out – it will be something else's turn.'

She really was feeling more robust.

'This is Robin's area,' Ian said. 'Robin? Robbo?'

He called to their son, who couldn't hear them above the music on his iPod.

'He reckons ants and cockroaches would be the only things to survive a nuclear future,' he said, revealing that Robin had talked to him about his theories too. Karen had shown him public information films on YouTube containing advice about how to make a nuclear shelter for the family out of tables and mattresses. As if hiding under a table could protect anyone against a searing nuclear blast.

She took Ian's hand and swung it, jovial, then brought it to her lips and kissed it.

'What was that for?' he asked, but she couldn't say. It would be too much like tempting fate to tell him that suddenly everything seemed possible. Instead, she proposed they get Indy a dog for her birthday.

'How about a bike?' Ian said. 'Fewer turds to pick up.'

'True.'

'Imagine it – all four of us cycling through the woods – how wholesome would that be?'

'You won't get Robin on a bike.'

'True.'

Back home she showed Indigo how to crumble flour, butter and sugar and the basement kitchen, warmed by the heat of the oven, grew fragrant with cinnamon and cloves. Fairy-lights glowed around the misted window that ran with condensation. After dinner she sat at the table reading the Sunday paper while the others were upstairs, elsewhere. Occasionally, she and Ian still talked about travelling or about moving to the country and getting a place with a bigger garden, but at times like these she felt they had found their true home.

At last, she went to find him.

'Ten more minutes, Robin,' she said, standing in her son's bedroom doorway while he twitched in front of a gunsight on a computer screen.

Indigo was already in bed. 'I can't sleep.' It was her daughter's way of asking her to stroke her head.

'What, even after that big long walk?' Karen said, sitting on the bed. She combed her fingers through Indy's hair and scanned the grubby lilac-painted walls of the room, decorated with years' worth of her own artwork going right back to dried pasta collages made at nursery.

Drawings of mermaids and princesses crowded posters of Disney's versions cut out from comics. She would be nine on her birthday but she was growing up fast. The previous week she had asked for a Facebook account. Maybe instead of a bike or a dog they should give her a room makeover. Karen's gaze fell on the dressing-up trunk and, testing herself, she tried to recall its contents: as well as a Cinderella dress and a Snow White outfit and a selection of wands, there were handbags and scarves of her mother's that had been in Karen's own dressing-up box when she was a girl. Indigo didn't dress up any more. Soon it would be time to store the collection in the loft space above the landing, along with Robin's Lego, ready for the next generation. The idea of her children's children, and this image of the future skidding and unwinding like cotton off a reel, made her giddy. In the past, this vertiginous sensation could feel unmanageable, as if she stood on the brink of an abyss, teetering, the ground underneath her feet threatening to crumble and fall away. Now, though, as her fingers traced the contours of her daughter's skull, she felt calm. It wasn't a false stupor that she had experienced before, where no feeling seemed able to penetrate her surface; it was a true calm. Her foothold felt secure. She had found her place – in the universe, in her life, in this small town, in this cramped little house, sitting on her daughter's bed. Indigo's breathing slowed in sleep. She stood up and the bed creaked. She heard a murmured, 'Night, Mum,' as she tiptoed out.

In their bedroom, Ian watched her take off her make-up. 'I'm mad to cycle on the spot in a sweaty gym next to strangers when I could be thrashing through glorious English woodland with my family,' he said. 'Let's go to Bike World and buy a whole set.'

She laid her silver bangle on the chest, opened a drawer to fetch a clean nightdress.

'What do you think the collective noun for bikes is?' he asked. 'A "zeal", maybe?'

'An idiocy of bikes,' she replied.

Her nightie held the coolness of the pine drawer. Among her underclothes, the foil packet of white tablets. Not for the first time recently she wondered if she might discard it. She glanced at the wicker basket in the corner of the room. 'Shall I put my cap in?'

'Cor, wouldn't say no.'

Foreplay.

Afterwards, she padded to the bathroom and then back to bed, shivering with cold. She threw away the foil packet. She felt safe and strong. As if hiding under a table could protect anyone against a searing nuclear blast.

MY SHEETS AND PYJAMAS were wet every morning but I left my pissy things on the bed. At home if it happens, I wait until Robin's gone then put everything in the washing machine. When I get home from school Nan's washed and dried it and the bed's all made again so it looks like nothing's happened.

At Dad's I left the wet sheets on the bed. I didn't even mind the smell. I liked it. Nan asked if I wanted her to ask Dad if we could put a few things in the wash. I said No thanks and she didn't know what to say then. She was standing in my room while I was sitting on the floor with my iPad. The wall felt cold against my back. Indigo, she said, I think we should get your sheets and things washed. She said she hadn't seen a washing machine anywhere but she could take them to Dad if I didn't want to.

The wall was nice and cool and I was pretending to be a marble statue of me. I stayed still with my face really serious. Nan said Are you alright Indy but I didn't answer and I didn't move. She said my name in a sharp voice so I snapped back into life again. You're spending too much time on that thing, she said, meaning my iPad, you're getting addicted.

She started taking the sheets and everything off. Come along, let's get this lot sorted, she said, but then she sat on the edge of the bed and I could tell I was going to get a talk. There's a lot on offer in the new South Africa, she said, A lot of opportunities for people like your dad and not just people like him, either. Everyone. You've got to think what you want, though.

The washing machine was disguised as a cupboard – that's why Nan couldn't find it. She told Dad that I sometimes had a bit of trouble at night. I didn't care that he knew. It's stress-related, Nan said. Luckily Robin didn't hear because he had his headphones on. After we found the washing machine I wanted to play the drawing game on my iPad but Nan made me put it away and go outside.

Even though everyone says there's so much to do, there's not much and there's nowhere to go. It was too hot outside. Dad was on the phone to some customers who were coming on a golfing holiday and everyone else was lying around like they had melted. Even Tonyhog just wanted to lie in the shade with the chickens. I spied on Zami who was with Lindisizwe and the skinny stick man outside the gate. It looked as if they were having an argument but I couldn't tell because they were talking in a foreign language. The stick man was waving around a bit like as if he was drunk. When Zami saw me he gave me a sad look. Then again his look is always sad.

I went in Dad's room and tried on some of the necklaces hanging on the wardrobe door and I took some money I found on the table, even though I knew it was stealing. When I look at the paintings in his house I can't remember what they were like when I first saw them. I thought they were just blobs of paint then, but now all I can see is the people. I stared and stared at the one in his bedroom, trying to make it blobs again.

THE BABY WAS TEN DAYS OLD and she still didn't have a name. For Karen it summed up the chaos they were in.

'She'll have a name soon enough,' Ian said. 'Robin wants to call her Fluff.'

Every day he brought her their son's latest suggestion, like a cat bringing a dead bird into the house.

'Are you going to be okay?' he asked, pulling on his jacket. It was his first day back at work.

She let out a sound and he stopped getting ready and came to sit on the bed. 'I don't know why we don't ask your parents,' he said.

She let her head drop forward over the baby at her breast. She couldn't speak.

'If we tell them we need help, Karen…' He parted the curtain of her hair and took their daughter's hand in his, studying her delicate fingers.

'Where's Robin?' she managed to ask eventually.

'I put the TV on.'

They both listened to the sounds coming from downstairs.

'Let's ask them at least,' Ian said. 'Give your mum a ring. If you don't, I will.'

He made her promise she would call her mother and he stood up from the bed, ready to leave. 'I love you,' he said.

'How's little Grace?' asked her mother when she telephoned later that afternoon.

'It's not Gracie yet, Mum, not for sure,' Karen said, looking down at the baby at her breast.

'Well, what's she called, then? Poor little thing needs

a name! And nothing too wacky, Karen. She'll have to live with it for the rest of her life. I liked Grace – Grace is nice. Is she a good little girl, do you think?'

'Of course she's good, Mum.'

'And is she feeding alright?'

'Yes, fine.'

'My milk wasn't enough for you,' her mother said. 'You wanted the good stuff.'

'I'm sure your milk was fine, Mum.'

'I used to put an extra spoonful in – of the powder, you know, that you use to make up the bottles. You were such a skinny little thing, always crying.'

It felt like an accusation.

'Of course, it meant your dad could feed you, so it was good in one way. Probably why you were always Daddy's girl.'

'Was I then?'

'Daddy's girl? I think so, don't you? I never got a look-in.'

There was another silence.

'Do you think it was because of... you know, was I closer to Dad after... that time?'

'Possibly.'

'We've never talked about it.'

'Yes, well, your generation are all for talking, that's your way of doing things.'

'I can't stop crying,' she said.

'You'll feel better in a few days. It's just a touch of the post-natals.'

'It's not that, Mum.'

'Baby blues, we used to call it – it's normal, what with all the hormones whizzing around. You'll feel better in a few days.'

'You're not listening,' Karen said, panic rising. 'I'm not normal.'

'What are you talking about?' her mother said, and Karen could picture her sitting at the tiny table in the hallway of her home, the outside world blurred through the distorting glass of the front porch. 'Of course you're normal! We're the most normal people I know.'

'I'm not coping,' she said. Her voice cracked and she felt her mother shift away from her at the other end of the telephone line, as if in that instant extra miles of cable were placed between them, looped and coiled and knotted in places, stretched to breaking point at others. Not for the first time, she became aware of how her parents struggled with the way she experienced the world. It pained her to know that her mother found it as hard as she did.

'You've got to admit…' her mother said, her voice confident, strident even, as if she was compensating for the extra distance that was suddenly between them. 'You have to admit there's a dissatisfaction in your generation, isn't there?'

Karen didn't answer. She wished her mother would speak truthfully instead of cloaking the conversation in speculation about generational difference.

'All the travelling you and Ian did,' she continued. 'I'm not sure it helps.'

Karen closed her eyes and, at the other end of the phone line, Valerie caught a whiff of her daughter's resistance.

'Does he know?' she asked.

Even though she couldn't see her, Karen shook her head. Her mother thought she endlessly wanted to talk about everything, but there were some things that couldn't be said.

'It might be as well to tell him. He has a right to know.'

Both women listened to the sounds of other things around them. Valerie could hear voices from next door's radio coming through the wall, while Karen listened to her baby's barely audible breathing and the sound of the television downstairs.

'Not that this is the same thing,' Valerie added.

'How do you know?' Karen asked.

IN THE CODE I MADE with Zami, shining for a long time then off then on again means you're happy. Shining for only two counts then off and on again means sad. It was dark and I was doing our code out of my window but Zami didn't do it back so I went to his shed to say why didn't you shine back. I had to creep quietly in case Dad heard me.

He was copying the words in Robin's guidebook as per usual and his writing made me want to scribble all over the page. I wanted to tear it out and screw it up, stuff it in my mouth, chew it then spit it out. If I did, he would just look at me in his usual way. When he stares at me I never know what he's thinking.

For an experiment, I picked up his exercise book and threw it on the floor. What's the point of all this, I said. He picked it up. I said Who is that skinny guy you talk to outside the gate, the one in the woolly hat – is he a friend of yours? It is no one, he said. A mosquito was humming next to my ear. Come on then, I said, and Zami said Where to? To see Young Lady, I said. It's good practice if you want to get a job with tourists.

He looked out of the window of his shed at the house where all the lights were on, then he looked at me. Without saying anything he stood up and took a shirt off a nail in the wall. He put the shirt on over his T-shirt. He put on some old trainers that went on his feet without undoing the laces, like a pair of slippers. We went outside and he shut the door of his shed. Jack started barking but Zami spoke in his calm voice and he stopped. Another dog started barking somewhere else far away. Zami said Wait here while I open the gate. I felt a bit sick. Are we going then, I asked, and he looked at me without smiling and said If you want to. I said Of course I want to.

The lights all around the house made big shadows. It was so cold my teeth were chattering. Zami was talking to Lindisizwe while I got in the Jeep. I was shivering but not just from the cold. It was really noisy when Zami started the engine but we drove fast. We drove so fast out of the gate I had to hold on tight to the sides. I looked behind to see if Dad was following us but my hair was in my face and eyes and all I could see was Lindisizwe dragging the gate shut.

DOUG AND VALERIE sat next to their daughter's bed, waiting for her to wake up. She was out of danger. They would be allowed to take her home later that day.

'Is she really asleep, do you think?' Valerie asked.

Doug didn't answer.

'She woke up alright when the doctor came round,' she said.

It was clear Karen didn't want to talk to them. She was prepared to speak to complete strangers – doctors and nurses she had never met before – but not to her own flesh and blood.

'You heard what the nurse said,' Doug whispered. 'After what her body's been through, sleep is the best thing for her.'

'Ironic, when you think about it,' Valerie said. She pressed her lips together, not wanting to say something she would regret.

The last time all three of them waited to be discharged from this same hospital had been when Karen was born, seventeen years ago. Then, as now, they had seen the sun rise. Today it was swollen and red, and so large that it filled the window of the hospital ward, lighting the room a rosy pink. Shepherd's warning, Valerie thought, but again, she stopped herself before opening her mouth to speak. 'She'll need clothes to travel home in, won't she?' she said instead.

'I'll go,' Doug said.

'No, you stay. I know what to bring. I know where everything is.'

'Will you be alright driving?'

'I'll be alright.'

She didn't like driving, but she didn't want to be the one sitting by the bed when Karen woke up. The nurses would be there, of course, and they were very nice, she couldn't fault them, but it was better if Doug stayed.

She followed his instructions and found their car where he had parked it the night before but she couldn't get the door open, the key wouldn't fit. She turned it this way and that, tried it upside down, even checked the numberplate, thinking she had the wrong car, although she was certain it was theirs because there was Doug's wooden-bead cover on the driver's seat. Her hands were shaking. This wasn't her; none of this was her. It wasn't how she pictured herself and her family. Finally she fumbled the key in the lock and got the door open. Once inside the car, she rested her forehead on the steering wheel and wept.

The traffic wasn't too heavy and she drove carefully

around the roundabout that always gave Doug trouble, allowing herself two complete circuits to make sure she got the right exit and didn't land up on the dual carriageway. The house seemed different on her return – transformed, somehow, by the events of the night before. She let herself in quickly, knowing that Shirley opposite would be watching.

Upstairs, she stood in the doorway of the bathroom. There had been no time to clean up the mess. She tried to conjure Karen on the floor again, lifeless and heavy as an oversized doll. The shrillness in Doug's voice as he'd shouted for her to call an ambulance had been more like a woman's scream than her husband's voice. She half wanted to see them again like that, the two of them – Karen gathered in her father's arms with the whites of her eyes showing and sick all down her front – and half wanted to scorch the image from her mind so she would never remember it. There was something extreme about what had happened, and they weren't extreme people. At least, she and Doug weren't. They kept themselves to themselves. They were polite, of course they were, but they liked things private, not like some.

She filled a bucket and fetched a scrubbing brush. Bleach fumes made her light-headed as she worked away at the bathroom carpet. She tried to summon details of their normal life: the setting of the morning alarm and the making of Doug's cup of tea while Karen got ready. They would have to let the school know. The hospital would make a follow-up appointment with their GP. She felt exposed, and it was hard not to blame Karen for exposing them. Other people might think of her as stuck-up but she wasn't. She was more private, perhaps, than some, and not one to wear her feelings on her sleeve. Of course she liked things to be a certain way – who didn't? – but she wasn't a snob. She emptied the bucket down the toilet. It was the way of the world, she thought: we get the children we deserve. The ones who will teach us how to be. Perhaps it was part of God's plan. She refilled her bucket with hot water. Margie and Dave Lawrence were what she would call extrovert, not to say highly strung (her, certainly) and yet their children, a girl and a boy, both appeared very sensible.

She emptied her bucket again and placed a towel over the stain, marching up and down on it to dry the offending patch. What to tell Shirley, who had watched out of her window as the ambulance crew lifted Karen into their vehicle? Best not to say anything at all.

She threw the towel away in the outside dustbin and went back upstairs. In Karen's room, the disinfectant smells wafting along the corridor from the bathroom couldn't overpower the scent of her daughter. She sat on the bed and looked out of the window. Next door's cat pawed the soil in Doug's flowerbed. The thought of rushing downstairs and out of the back door to clatter the saucepan she kept on the worktop for the purpose made her feel tired. She thought about laying her head on the pillow but her daughter's smell was overwhelming. On the one hand she was repelled by it and on the other she feared that, if she surrendered to it, she could drift into a deep sleep from which she might never awake.

'Come on, Val,' she said out loud.

She parcelled up the navy padded jacket Karen wore every day and selected a jumper and skirt and fresh underwear from the drawers. She packed the garments in the Weekender bag that Doug used for business trips and placed Karen's Chinese slippers on the top. The cloth they were made from was so thin they were hardly shoes at all, yet she wore them in all weathers. They held the shape of her feet, bearing imprints of her toes where they pressed.

She drove back to the hospital, where Karen was still sleeping, supposedly.

'She woke up and said hello,' Doug said, 'and then she went back to sleep again.'

Valerie folded the clothes over the end of the bed and placed the Chinese slippers neatly side by side on the floor underneath. She got Doug to write in a card addressed to *A Dear Daughter* and stood it on the bedside cabinet so Karen would see it when she woke up.

They would be glad to be home again, after such a long night and after all this hanging around, but she couldn't imagine how they would be with each other away from the careful, serious doctors and away from the nurses with their bright faces. She felt almost embarrassed to think about it. Maybe there would be a wildlife programme or a comedy on television that they could watch together. They would have an early night. Valerie wouldn't sleep, however. She would be awake forever, now. She was exhausted, but it wasn't the kind of tiredness she could sleep off. It was a different kind of tired. One thing was certain: she wouldn't be taking any sleeping tablets. She blamed Doug for even having them in the house. Look what happened.

WHEN WE HAD BEEN driving for a while Zami stopped. It was so cold we had to put on some of the old clothes and blankets from under the back seat of the Jeep. They smelled like Nan's winter coat. Zami showed his ID to the man in the shed but the man kept saying It's not allowed. He walked around to my side of the Jeep and I was glad I had my alarm under the blanket. Zami said we had to go back but then I had the idea of showing the money I got from Dad's room. The man shone his torch at it. He took it out of my hand and counted it and then he waved his hand and we were allowed to drive into the park. He didn't give me any change.

We drove on the rough track for a little way and then Zami stopped to listen. There was a kind of moaning. The headlights shone in a straight line in front of us, lighting up a clump of bushes in the distance and a slope running down from where we were to a plain stretch of land. We were in the middle of nowhere. The moaning stopped and then started again, stopped and then started. Zami said it was a lion but it didn't sound like one to me. I didn't know what it was but it didn't sound like a lion. Zami switched off the engine and let the Jeep roll down a little slope so we wouldn't make any noise. It was so bumpy I had to hold on to the side to stop myself being thrown out.

At the bottom of the slope the Jeep stopped rolling and we heard more moans. Zami switched off the lights and we were in complete darkness. I held his hand and he didn't take it away. His fingers felt dry. It was quiet all around, but a full kind of quiet, as if someone was lying in wait, holding their breath. Then whatever it was couldn't hold on any longer. A horrible cackling like a witch made me jump. Hyenas. They weren't as loud as the woman screaming on my alarm but their sound was much worse. Zami said it meant there could be a kill nearby – antelope most probably. He was being like a proper safari leader but the thought of a dead antelope with hyenas all over it made me want to be back at Dad's house. Let's go, I said. We can come back with Dad and Robin tomorrow and show them. I thought you wanted to see Young Lady, Zami said, but I told him I had changed my mind. But if I get out to start the engine the lions will eat me, he said. Even though it was dark I could hear in his voice that he was smiling when he said it so I said You should have thought of that, shouldn't you? Joking made me feel less scared and we were still holding hands but then he let go and jumped out. When

I called his name his voice came from round the front of the Jeep where he was starting the engine. I didn't know if a lion or a hyena would be scared of my alarm so I patted all around me like a blind person, trying to find a weapon. If Zami got mauled I could probably drive, from what he showed me and from watching Dad, but only if he got the engine started before he was attacked. He would have to tell me what to do, but he couldn't do that if he was unconscious or if half his face was eaten off.

The engine kept clicking without turning on and the hyenas were making their horrible noise. It sounded as if there were lots of them all climbing on the dead antelope, tearing its guts out and shrieking. I tried to tell Zami to get back in but the night swallowed up my voice and nothing came out. Then the Jeep gave a bounce as he climbed back in. No petrol, he said, and I started to get scared. Stop mucking about, I said. Put the lights back on. He said we needed to save the battery. Put them on, I said, I mean it. I sounded like Robin.

Zami turned the lights on and we saw pale shapes moving softly and slowly against the dark. Lions. They arrived out of nowhere, like ghosts, a male and four females. This time it was Zami who held my hand, not the other way round.

We were quiet for ages, watching and waiting to see what they would do. I was thinking that our Jeep had no sides or roof or petrol and I didn't tell Dad or Nan where I was going. My chest grew tight as if the blanket around me was a boa constrictor but I didn't cry. Then Zami said You want to go now? How can we, I said, and my voice was all croaky. I thought we would be stuck there all night until Dad or the man in the shed came looking for us and found our mangled bodies with lion claw marks in and hyenas scavenging all over.

Zami jumped down from the Jeep and the nearest lion looked at him. He lifted up the bonnet. The headlights lit him up bright and the lions were fainter behind. I remembered what Robin said about how if there was a kill they wouldn't be hungry but the lion could easily run across and leap on to his back and attack him just for fun. Her heavy paws would pull him to the ground and her claws would shred his shirt and his flesh. Also, it was the hyenas who were eating the kill so maybe the lions weren't full. Maybe they had room for Zami. His face was even more serious than normal while he was looking at the engine. He told me to turn the key and when I did the engine roared. The big male lion jumped up and the others ran away into the shadows when Zami slammed the bonnet.

The wheels made a horrible noise when we went back up the little hill, with rocks flying everywhere and the tyres skidding like in an action film. Once we got away I wanted to shout and scream. I stood up while we were driving along, holding on to the frame and screaming with my head sticking out of the top so my hair blew about and I got brain freeze. I was louder than my Alarm Girl, louder than Beth on a rollercoaster and I didn't stop. I wanted Zami to shout too but he wouldn't. He was laughing at me. I love the sound of his laugh.

HER MOTHER ASKED if she wanted to say goodbye to the home where she'd grown up. Karen didn't feel the need but it seemed important to her parents. On the train journey she read the guidebook that Ian had annotated. He had scribbled 'sounds good!' in green biro next to descriptions of sites of interest and 'don't mind if we do' next to hostels where they might stay. It felt like a conversation, as if he was sitting on the train next to her. One of the pages contained a photograph of a hilltop Nepalese temple, against which he had written 'wow'.

The places described in the book felt remote from the town where her parents lived – more distant even than the actual number of miles separating them – so as the train sped out of the city and towards the suburbs this dialogue of theirs was a comfort. She leaned her forehead against the window and dreamed of their escape while urban sprawl, with its playgrounds and industrial estates, gave way to wasteland and then fields. Farm buildings flashed past, then a small town, then fields once more.

She saw no one on the walk from the train station to her old house. In India the streets would be thronging, the streets crammed with cars and motorbikes hooting their horns. A solitary vehicle passed by, its driver looking straight ahead, ignoring her lone figure, tyres hissing on the wet road. Everyone else was indoors, behind lighted windows with curtains drawn. She passed a house where she could see into the front room. A woman was serving up dinner to young children. Karen shuddered.

Even with the distraction and business of the house move, her mother interrogated her about her plans, just as Karen had known she would.

'Where will you stay?' she asked as they stood in the middle of the empty bedroom that had once been hers. Karen's father dismantled a wardrobe, laying its pieces in a neat pile under the window.

'We're taking a tent,' Karen said, but she couldn't resist adding, 'but it will be hot enough to sleep out if we want. Some people just sleep on the beach.'

She knew she was being cruel.

'Under the stars! Romantic!' her father said.

He could be cruel too.

'How safe is it to visit these countries?' her mother asked.

'I'll be fine, Mum, everyone does it.'

She inserted the toe of her boot in a dent in the carpet where her bed had stood.

'Remember the first time you stayed in the tent instead of in the caravan with us?' her father said. 'What was that girl's name?'

'What girl?' her mother asked.

'Kaz brought a friend with her that year we went to Devon.'

'Did I?'

'Yes! Nicola something.' He gathered up the pieces of wardrobe and edged out of the door.

'Mind how you go,' her mother said as he headed down the stairs.

'Angela, not Nicola. Angela Knight!' Karen called after him.

'Now what about this little lot?' Her mother gestured at a pile of random objects gathered in the middle of the floor. A jewellery box, a painted pebble, a broken hairdryer.

'It's only bits and pieces, Mum.'

She picked up a doll from the pile. It wore French regional costume and had watched her from the windowsill for years with its badly painted eyes.

'We've got a lorry full of bits and pieces! I need you to take what's yours.'

Sunlight had bleached its red cape and, during boring stints of homework, Karen had chewed its plastic feet into frayed, shapeless stumps. She was seized by nostalgia and the surge felt dangerous – vertiginous, almost. Something about the pathetic pile and her mother's concern overtook her, and it was something, too, about being back in this house. Maybe it was haunted. She shuddered again, as she had when she'd first arrived, with a sense of something or someone at her shoulder, breathing hot breath in her ear. She could almost smell it.

'I don't know what to do with any of this,' she said, tossing the doll back on to the pile. It lay face-up, staring at her with blobs for eyes. 'Don't ask me to throw it away.'

'No one's saying it has to be thrown away,' her mother said. 'Why must you be so dramatic?'

'This is our life,' she said, feeling panicky.

'Did I tell you we got thirty pounds for the sofa?' her mother asked.

'I can't bear to think about someone else sitting on our sofa!'

'It was a horrid old thing.'

She felt her mother's eyes on her.

'You're going with this Ian, are you?' she asked.

'What do you mean, "this Ian"? You said you liked him.'

'You've got a nice little job... Are you sure you want to give that up?'

'It's not a "nice little job", Mum – I was only ever doing it to save up money to go travelling.'

'How about buying somewhere?' Her mother followed her on to the landing.

'A semi on the south coast, d'you mean? I'd end up killing myself.'

She regretted her words as soon as they were out of her mouth, and couldn't help glancing into the bathroom, where the mat had been removed, revealing a stain on the pale carpet. 'What are we doing empty-handed?' her mother said quickly, returning to the bedroom. Karen heard her gather up clothes-hangers with a clatter.

It was safer downstairs, but her mother kept picking at her plans. 'You think you'll travel well together, do you? Ian knows you, does he?'

'He knows me as well as anyone knows anyone else, Mum. Do you and Dad know everything there is to know about each other?'

'I should hope so, after nearly forty-five years of marriage!' her father said.

It was getting dark. She helped load their car under the yellow light cast by the lamps either side of the driveway.

'It's best to be certain, though, isn't it?' her mother persisted. 'You hear about these couples who go away on trips and they only last a few weeks before they can't stand the sight of one another.'

'That won't happen to us,' Karen said.

'Have you told him?' her mother asked in a low voice.

'Told him what?' She would make her say it.

'About that time. Hospital... and what... took you there.'

'There's no need. That was ages ago.'

They returned to the house.

'And you're happy, Karen? Would you say you're happy?'

'I'm happy, Mum, yes. You don't need to worry.'

For a brief moment she felt a tenderness towards her parents, and was sorry for what she had put them through. 'How about you and Dad?' she asked. 'How are you about moving and stuff?'

'Oh, we're alright,' her mother replied. 'On with the new, don't look back.'

They ate a Chinese takeaway in the empty kitchen and by evening they were gone. Countryside flashed past the train windows in the dark and Karen wondered what Angela Knight was doing now. On the last day of their Devon holiday, her parents helped them take their tent down. It tugged in the wind as they released its guy ropes, billowing and flapping at first, then floating softly down when the poles were removed. When they removed the groundsheet, a patch of yellow grass marked where they had been.

IT TOOK AGES to get back to the house. All the lights made it look like a bright city. Lindisizwe and Zami had a long talk in their foreign language. When I asked Zami what they were saying he just shrugged. I said Now I know how to drive and where to go for spotting lions the next thing you can teach me is African swear words. While we were waiting for the gates to open, I asked him if we really broke down back where the lions were. He looked at me with his sorrowful eyes. Nan says I have got a ferocious stare that is too serious for a young girl but she should see Zami's. He is a boy, though, so maybe she wouldn't mind it so much. While he was looking at me I thought he could be tricking me about breaking down. Not nice, I said, and I smacked him. He said Hitting is what is not nice and he rubbed his arm, even though my smack was only a joke one, not hard. How about driving into a load of lions and pretending to have no petrol, I said, that's not nice, but he stayed serious and said again that hitting wasn't nice for a young girl. When he said girl he pronounced it gel. I made him say it again. It's girl, not gel, I said. He said Okay, girl, and he was smiling.

We drove into the yard and Tonyhog came trotting round from behind the house. He looked so cute, like he thought he was really important, with his tail straight up in the air. I said Go away, Tony, it's way past your bedtime. Jack ran out of his kennel and started barking. He pulled his chain tight and wouldn't stop barking. Then there was a man in front of us. It was the stick man and he had a stick. He was wearing Zami's Manchester City shirt. He grabbed Zami and pulled him out of the Jeep. He was speaking in his foreign language and his face was shiny in the night. He was angry and hissing, kind of, and he was hitting and dragging Zami. I shouted at him and when he looked at me he was like a demon not a man. His eyes seemed like they would pop out of his head and he was shaking Zami so I pulled out the pin of my alarm. The girl's screams pierced my ears. Dad came out of the house shouting my name and the man looked round. I'm armed, Dad said, and he waved his stun gun in the air. Zami was on the ground trying not to get hit and Jack was going mad barking. Alarm Girl was screaming. The Jeep engine was still going so I got in the driving seat and pressed the pedal. The Jeep jerked forward and the man had to let go of Zami and jump out of my way. Zami ran out of the gate. Dad shouted at me but I knew what to do. I put the gearstick into reverse and stamped on the pedal. There was a loud bump and a screeching noise so I shoved the gearstick again and drove forward but this time I crashed into the garage wall. A sheet of metal slid off the roof and clanged on the ground. There was a horrible screeching but even when I put the pin back in my alarm it didn't stop. Someone else ran out of the house. It was Grandad, running quite fast. I could see Robin and Nan pressed up against the window watching from inside. Dad got me out of the Jeep. My legs were shaking so much I couldn't walk, he had to make me. Don't turn around, he said, but I didn't know what he was talking about so I looked back and I saw Grandad was holding Tonyhog. Tony's legs were jerking. It was him screaming. His screams ripped the night apart. I pushed Dad away, even though he tried to keep hold of me. Grandad said Get her away from here, Ian, but I fought Dad when he tried to make me. Don't look then, he said, and he put his gun next to Tony's head and shot him. The screaming stopped. He's only stunned, Dad said, and he walked over and picked up one of the painted white rocks around the tree. He hit Tony on the head with it, and then he did it again.

Three hits and then we knew Tony was dead. Now it was me screaming but Grandad just stood still. Dad said It had to be done, Indy. I knew I was next. I ran around the front of the Jeep to get away from him. Kill me then if you're going to, I said. Kill me like you killed Tony and you killed Mum! Robin had come out of the house by then and he shouted Leave Dad alone. We were all in the yard apart from Nan who was the only one still in the house. The rest of us were all in the yard with me and Robin shouting and Tonyhog dead on the ground.

KAREN SAT AT THE TABLE in the basement kitchen, wrapping presents. The room was quiet. The gift-wrap had a repeating pattern of squirrels and other woodland animals. She folded it around books and DVDs she had chosen, around a T-shirt with a kitten print, size 9–10 years. Ian would be back from the gym soon. He would bring the main present, a bicycle.

She paused in her task for a moment, lifting her nose to sniff the night air. It smelled like summer but it wasn't even spring yet. She placed both her hands on the table top and looked carefully around the room. It felt to her as if someone else had arranged its contents and yet she knew it was she who had wound fairy-lights around the window frame. The room felt touched by something outside of herself, though, while she, estranged, sat in the middle of it.

She scraped her chair abruptly away from the table and got up to open the back door. A blackbird flew out of the tree next door, trilling shrilly as it went. A smell of greenness and newness filled her nostrils and she leaned against the house for support. The night was like a well. She took several deep breaths, feeling she might drown.

A door banged, seemingly far away. She heard her husband's tread on the stairs as he came into the room where the presents lay wrapped.

'Karen?' He found her. 'What are you doing?'

She kept her face turned away as she answered him. 'It's an amazing evening.'

He waited for something further while she wondered if he could feel what she could feel – a presence clinging thickly to objects and surfaces. He went to the sink to get himself a glass of water.

'Where d'you want the bike?' he said, above the rush of water from the tap. 'Shall we put it down here with the rest?'

'Okay.'

Oblivious to the effort it took her to utter two syllables, he emptied the glass and crashed it noisily on to the draining board. He bounded back up the stairs and went to fetch the bicycle.

She pushed off the wall, like a swimmer away from the edge of a pool, and stepped gingerly back indoors. The digital display on the microwave read 21:54. She got down on her knees.

'What are you doing?'

He was back already. She looked up at him from her kneeling position, feeling the harsh fibres of the back doormat prickle through the denim of her jeans.

'Nine years ago I was giving birth,' she said. 'At exactly this time, in this position.'

Her words sounded strange to her and she wasn't surprised that he gave her a peculiar look. He wheeled the bike across the room to lean it against the table.

'Are you going to the supermarket? I'll park the car if not.'

She got to her feet. 'I'm going, yes.'

He held out the car keys and she took them. Lifting her handbag off a chair as she went, she clicked the front door shut behind her.

He had left the car headlights on. Their beam was sinister, like a border control searchlight, challenging fugitives to enter its glare. A fox emerged from bins at the end of the road. It held her stare for a moment before trotting quickly away. She looked up and down the street. Her neighbours' houses stared back with blank faces. The public front of her own house seemed like a different country compared with the intimacy of its back patio, invaded only by the visiting blackbird. Her senses were tingling but she couldn't tell if she was excited or nervous, or something else entirely. She was afraid of the uncertainty of the feeling. It was a kind of animal instinct, like the fox's or the blackbird's, alerting her to the approach of whatever it was that she could feel beginning to move in on her.

She got inside the car and locked the driver's door. Resting her hands on the steering wheel for a moment, she checked the back seat, testing to make sure she was alone, so strong was the feeling that she was in company. It was her child's birthday tomorrow, she told herself. She said it out loud. 'I have wrapped the presents and now I will buy food.' Her voice sounded strange, with just herself to hear it.

She spoke calmly and firmly, as if she was at the scene of a disaster or an emergency, but the sensation that she was not alone would not leave her. There was something crouching in the passenger seat, writhing silently and vigorously around her feet. It insinuated itself next to her, cloaked itself around her, and now, as she turned the key in the ignition, it was coming shopping with her.

DAD SAID WHAT WERE you doing out here but I only wanted to know where Zami was. Dad said Were you with him? Where have you been? They didn't even know I had gone. All the time I was at the lions they thought I was in bed. When I said Me and Zami went out in the Jeep Dad shouted What did he do to you? I shouted back Nothing! Get away from me! He said he was going to phone the police. Grandad said for everyone to stay calm and get back inside the house but I didn't want to leave Tony. His human eyes were open but his head was lying on one side in a weird way and blood was coming out from under his body. Dad couldn't shut the gate because he forgot the code. He had to go indoors where it was written down. Lindisizwe was gone, so was Zami and so was the stick man. Grandad wanted me and Robin to go indoors but I wouldn't leave Tonyhog. Grandad said There's nothing we can do for the poor fellow and he covered his body up with the Jeep blanket.

Dad was already on the phone to the police when we came inside. My whole body was shivering and I couldn't stop my teeth from chattering. Nan gave me my hoody but every bit of me couldn't stop shaking. When Robin heard Dad say to the police he had no idea who the intruder was he looked at me and said Was that Zami's sister's husband? I didn't know. Robin told Dad how we had been to Zami's sister's house. Dad said You went on the bus by yourselves? I said No, we were with Zami. Nan said she felt sick. The police will be here any minute, Dad said to Robin, you need to tell them everything you've just told me. As for you, young lady, you've got some explaining to do. You can either tell me now or when the police get here. I said You're the one the police will be interested in and he said What do you mean, Indy and he made his voice go all gentle like when we were little. His gentle voice made tears gush out of my eyes and the words came tumbling after. I said How about you? You're the one with explaining to do. How could you do it? How could you do it? Dad said Do what, Indy? I don't know what you're talking about. He wanted to hold my hand and Grandad wanted to get near me too but I wouldn't let them, I just stood in the middle of all of them like I was on my own and they were the world. There was a confused look on all the grown-ups' faces, like on the sacrificed chicken's and like on poor Tony's. The thought of Tony made me cry even more and once I started I couldn't stop. It all came out: how I killed Tony and Dad killed you. The words came out of my mouth as fast as the tears out of my eyes. I said Nan, why didn't you tell us? How can you keep something like that a secret? You know it, Grandad knows it – why did you make us come to South Africa to live with a murderer? Robin said What are you talking about so I shouted at him Don't pretend you don't know but he just looked at me and his face was all twisted up.

Everyone was really quiet when I stopped saying it and they were all looking at me. Dad said Christ, Valerie. Everything was calm then. I felt calm too, even though it was the worst night of my whole life, even worse than the night of my birthday when you weren't there because you were dead.

Dad put both his hands on my shoulders and looked at me right in the face. I could smell his breath. Then he let go and he said something to Nan and Grandad about the trouble with not telling me and I could tell by their voices that they were talking about you. Grandad said I was too young to understand. His voice was even quieter than normal. Then Dad's voice got quite loud. He said Look what she thinks instead! He held my shoulders again, really tight this time and said But not really, eh, Indy? You don't really think I killed Mummy, he said. I didn't say anything back because he called you Mummy not Mum and that made me cry.

Nobody talked to me or came near me. There was a space around me, as if I had a disease that was catching. There was a disgusting feeling all around, a bit like at your funeral when I felt car-sick the whole time even though I wasn't in a car. The disgusting feeling was because of the night and the lemony smell of the mosquito candles and because of the stick man fighting Zami and because of Tonyhog. Sometimes when the feeling in the room isn't right I just want it to be normal but now I wanted it to stay like it was because it felt right to feel so horrible. Everything was horrible and everyone was feeling horrible so it was good that it stayed that way even though the feeling itself was horrible.

KAREN DROVE TO THE outskirts of the town. The bus stops were deserted, even though it was only ten o'clock. She drove over the roundabout and into the industrial estate. The woodland flanking the darkened buildings was still and quiet. The supermarket glowed like a citadel, its luminous twenty-four-hour petrol station tinting the night sky yellow.

Inside the shop she trawled the aisles, filling her trolley at a leisurely pace. A packet of biscuits was balanced on top of the other items in her trolley, and something about the way it teetered on the pile moved Karen. The image on the packet showed the different coloured icing on wafers, and the inadequacy of the representation, coupled with the certain knowledge that the biscuits themselves were no better than the picture, winded her. The paleness of the yellow icing and the indeterminate nature of the pink were too insubstantial to tolerate. The biscuits could only disappoint, and, as she stood in the brightly lit supermarket aisle, this seemed true of everything.

She and Ian had travelled the world. They had climbed Kilimanjaro and swum off the Great Barrier Reef. Yet she had brought them back to this ugly little corner of the planet. She put the biscuits more securely in the trolley and tried to carry on. There were good reasons why she was shopping at a late-night supermarket in the middle of a dull industrial estate in England. It was her daughter's birthday the next day.

She couldn't help glancing at the biscuit packet again. The brown icing was bad, too, like the worst cup of coffee possible in icing form and suggestive of all that was weak and bitter in the world. She knew it was foolish to be so affected by a food packaging design but she felt powerless in the face of what it implied about the sheer hopelessness of human enterprise.

She looked up to the ceiling, wanting to burn out her eyes in the glare of the overhead strip-lighting. If it were daytime she would go outside and stare into the sun. She gripped the supermarket trolley and pushed it forward a few feet, trying to resist the force pressing against her skull from the inside and trying to think about beautiful things. But the woodland walk of only a few weeks ago was forgotten. The delicate winter light forgotten. Her children's vigour as they thrashed through undergrowth with sticks in the pale afternoon, forgotten. Her husband's tenderness as he took her hand on the path and later that night as he caressed her, all forgotten.

She made a mental list of beautiful places she had been but could only think that she was too ugly for those places. She was the ugliest entity on the planet – not wicked or cruel, but possibly something worse: a negative, draining what was positive around her. In a bid to remain rational, she dared to recall attempts of hers over the years to locate the origins of this feeling of unworthiness. A doctor she had seen suggested that it might be a purely chemical issue, an imbalance in her brain chemistry. That was Ian's theory too. He had been immeasurably patient and loving, urging her to accept her condition. 'Don't fight yourself,' he said. 'You won't win.' She was frightened she might have transferred her curse to Robin and Indigo, via the placenta or in a poison secreted along with her breast milk. Even if they had managed not to ingest it, she thought, they would feel its impact, especially as they grew older. Her negative would drain their positive – there was no escape.

She loosened her fingers from the plastic of the trolley and sank to the floor. It was comforting to lay her cheek against the smooth, cool surface. A woman bent to address her.

'You alright, love?'

'I'm fine.'

'Want me to fetch someone?'

Karen got to her feet.

'Felt a bit faint, did you?' the woman asked.

'A bit, yes.'

'Happens to me all the time,' said the woman. 'My blood pressure's terrible.'

The woman moved off. Karen turned in the other direction. She walked briskly through the supermarket, leaving behind the iced biscuits in their incriminating packet. She walked past the cashiers chatting at their tills and into the black night.

THE POLICE CAME AND we had to tell them everything that happened. What about Tony, I said, and Dad said Never mind about Tony, Tony's dead. He made it seem to the police that Zami had done something bad by taking me on safari so late at night even though it was my idea. Robin told them about us going to Zami's sister's house. Nan was shaking her head while he was telling them. I told them how some African people think it's good luck to bury a baby under their new house and maybe the stick man was Zami's sister's husband and he wanted her baby as a sacrifice but the police didn't think so.

When they left, Dad asked who wanted a drink – hot chocolate or something stronger? Robin said something stronger. Nan started making hot chocolate but she was dropping things so Dad told her to come and sit down. He made everyone sit on the two sofas facing each other. Nan and Grandad were on one; me, Robin and Dad were on the other. Dad's hands were brown with Tonyhog's dried blood and his blood was on Grandad's shirt too. I asked if they were sure Tonyhog was dead and Dad said it was definite and we would have to bury him before the jackals came but he didn't want to talk about Tony, he wanted to talk about you.

Dad said You know Mum was ill and I said Yes. He said it was more of a sickness really. I don't know what's the difference between ill and sick, I said. I heard a noise outside that I thought might be jackals but Dad got angry and told me to forget about the bloody jackals. I couldn't forget about the jackals, though, and I couldn't forget about Tonyhog. He said you had a kind of sickness in your brain that meant you didn't feel normal and made you think you would be better off dead. I said At least she got her wish then but Robin shouted at me She killed herself you idiot.

Robin knew. He used to hear you crying. I never heard you. I never saw you.

I said to Robin Why didn't you tell me and he said What was I going to say – Mum's upset, go and make her better? Yes, I said but Robin just shook his head like I was some dumb kid.

Dad said no one could make you better. Your sadness was a feeling that nothing could stop. You had it for a long time. You got some medicine from the doctor but it didn't help. Nan said Well the tablets helped for a while, Ian, and her mouth went into a straight line after she said it. You've changed your tune, Valerie, Dad said – you were against antidepressants in the beginning. I saw how they helped her, Nan said. They didn't though, Dad said, not really. But she couldn't stop crying before, Nan said. She couldn't function! No one said anything and then Dad told us that you took medicine to make you better but the medicine made you feel like someone else instead of making you feel like yourself. When it made you better you stopped taking it but then you felt too much.

Grandad's face was covered with his hands. His shoulders were shaking. Nan was sitting next to him but she wasn't looking at him. I wanted to go over to him but it felt like I wasn't allowed to move from where I was.

Dad told us that he was in a group of people who were accusing the company that made your medicine because when you stopped taking it you felt even worse than you did before and you didn't want to feel like that again so you killed yourself. Grandad made a weird sound and Nan said Doug, you're upsetting the children. I went and sat next to him and he put his head against my shoulder and he accidentally called me Kaz, which was his name for you, I know. Robin came over and Nan had to move along because we were all squashed on one sofa. The other sofa was completely empty.

Dad said you tried to kill yourself when you were a teenager, too, when you were older than Robin but younger than a grown-up woman. Some people have that feeling inside of them all of the time. Luckily you were saved because you took too many pills but not quite enough. Grandad found you and saved you. Dad wasn't there because you weren't married and he didn't know you then.

Grandad was leaning on me really heavily and his crying was making my hoody all wet. It was like he was a different person because we had never seen him cry before. People look and sound like they're completely different people when they cry. Their crying self is a private one that no one sees and I had never seen Grandad's, not even at your funeral when I saw Dad and Nan and your friends crying. Me and Robin and Grandad were the only ones who didn't cry.

Dad crouched on the floor next to me and next to Robin and he said that we were different people from you and him and there was no reason why we should feel the same as you did when you were young. I asked how you did it, did you take enough pills this time? Nan said Yes but Dad said No more secrets Valerie and he told us you went to some woods and strangled yourself.

Grandad sat up and wiped his face when Dad said that. Him and Nan looked straight ahead, like they were statues. I tried looking at what they were looking at but it wasn't anything. They were just staring straight ahead. Dad was looking at me and it was as if he was looking for something but I didn't know what.

It was late at night, Dad said, with not many people about, and it was dark in the woods and you had a rope. You hanged yourself from a tree. A man was walking his dog the next morning and he found you hanging from the tree.

I didn't look at Robin when Dad was telling us and he didn't look at me. I asked what the man's name was but Dad didn't know who I was talking about. I meant the man who found you. Dad said he didn't know his name. I asked if he was at your funeral but Dad said no, he wasn't. He didn't know you. He was a stranger. It was the night before my birthday when I was nine and you went to the supermarket to get all the things for my party – all the party food and the paper plates – but you had a rope as well. It was in the car in case it broke down. You said to Dad that you were going to the shops and those were the last words anyone ever heard from your mouth.

Dad said there was nothing anybody could do about you dying and it was nobody's fault. He said he certainly didn't murder you and he didn't know where

I got that idea. This was the problem with not speaking about stuff, he said, and Robin said Why didn't you tell us? We knew already and Dad said I'm very very sorry about that, Robin, I made a mistake.

I didn't know.

I was thinking If only you hadn't died on my birthday. I started crying because I was thinking about the policewoman who came and did some drawing with me on that day and I was thinking about my red bike and how I never rode it much and how it was probably too small for me now.

THE PILOT GREETED his passengers and announced the temperature in Cape Town.

'Twenty-one degrees will do nicely,' said the woman sitting next to Ian.

The plane began to move slowly forward and he clasped his hands together. The woman gave him a sympathetic smile, perhaps assuming that he was a nervous flier.

He looked away.

The tremor of the engine shuddered in his chest as the plane took off. Out of the window, England, with both his children in it, tilted away. He had left them with their grandparents before, many times, while he was establishing the new life he was making for all of them, but it was a risk he was taking, making this move permanent. Fields and roads grew miniature as the plane climbed and were suddenly lost as they entered cloud. He would Skype every day as usual, but Robin and Indy could be strangers the next time he saw them. Their lifestyle with Val and Doug was so different from the one he and Karen had planned. Then again, nothing was as they'd planned.

'Your first trip to South Africa?' his fellow passenger asked once the seatbelt sign had been turned off. She unclipped her belt with manicured fingernails.

'No, I've been before,' Ian answered. He didn't return her question, and remembered a cardboard sign he'd made once for Indy to play shop with, with the words *Open* and *Closed* written on it.

He shut his eyes and leaned his head back against the headrest. Indy had a new habit of fidgeting with a scarf she carried about – a comfort blanket by any other name. Her grandmother called her 'Mrs Fiddle'. He had asked Valerie not to draw attention to the habit in this way, pointing out that Robin occasionally used the nickname against his sister, but Val told him it was harmless and that it was helpful for girls to have what she called 'their corners' knocked off by an older brother.

Indy dreamed about her mother and in the mornings, when she described the appearances her mother made during the night – calling to Indy from clifftops, standing watching her from doorways, forever on a threshold, it seemed – she would twist and twist her scarf. Ian wished Karen would come to him in his dreams, even just to call to him from a far clifftop. He wanted to hear her voice. He missed her.

IT WAS CLEAR AND COLD outside and even with the security lights there were loads of stars. The yard smelled of petrol. Tonyhog was on the ground next to the Jeep. There were tyre marks on the ground and blood was coming out from under the blanket that covered him. There were no lights on in Zami's shed. I asked Dad where he was and Dad said the village, probably. When he comes back, don't tell him off, I said, and I made Dad promise.

We had to make Tonyhog a grave otherwise the jackals would get him. The spade was heavy. Rust from its handle flaked off in my hand. We went to the far corner of the garden where the security lights were faintest and it was almost dark and we started to dig. Jack didn't bark and Dad said what a good guard dog he was because he only barked when something was wrong, like earlier when the horrible stick man was there. It made me shiver to think of the stick man's yellow eyes and his snake voice and his hitting.

I could dig up the grass easily but underneath it was earth so dry and hard we had to chip it with the pointed edges of our spades first. Soon we were making a hole. I said to Dad Maybe Zami's sister could come and live here and work for you like Zami does but he said it wasn't as simple as that. I asked him why not and he said People have their own lives and that he didn't have room in his life for a baby on top of everything else. Like you don't have room for us, I said, and that made him stop digging. He said of course he had room for us, wasn't he the one who wanted us to come and live with him? I told him I didn't want him and Beautiful to be girlfriend and boyfriend and he called me sweetheart like he was being kind but what he said wasn't kind. He said there were some things that weren't anything to do with me. Without the security lights it was dark so I couldn't see what his face looked like when he said it.

Grandad came out to help us and after ages the grave was ready. My hands were sore from holding the spade. We tried to carry Tony over to it but he was so heavy me and Grandad couldn't lift our end so Dad had to carry him by himself. He held him like a big baby. His body was warm like it was when he was alive and sunbathing with me and Zami scratching his back.

When Dad tipped Tony into the hole, a gasping noise came out of me, I couldn't help it. No one paid any attention to me crying and I was glad. Tony's poor tusks wouldn't fit so his neck got crooked at a funny angle and Dad had to push him in with both hands. He packed some straw around the body and then we shovelled all the earth back in and Dad said he would get some big rocks to put on top. Nan and Robin came out to help and we all got a rock each. Nan said be careful not to drop them because we could break our toes. Hers was the smallest rock, then mine, then Grandad's and Robin's were about the same size and Dad's was the biggest. In the end when we had done it we all stood around like at a funeral. Dad said Tony was one of the family. We were all standing there and it felt like we were all separate inside our family. I was separate and Dad and Robin and Nan and Grandad were all separate. You were separate from all of us. Tony had joined our family but in the end he was separate too, just a bushpig that had to be buried quickly so the jackals didn't get him.

You said I was looking very grown-up these days. I said it was because I had a tan and new shoes and a puffball skirt and you said it was true, all those things were the things that made me look more grown-up than when you last saw me. I asked where you'd been and you just said Away. I asked if you missed us and you said Yes of course, Go-Go. Why don't you come back then? You said you couldn't. You asked if I liked living at Nan and Grandad's and I said it was okay. It gets a bit annoying when Nan won't let me stay up late but Robin's allowed to, I said, and you said that's because Robin's older. I told you I don't like Grandad's smell in the morning and you laughed and asked me what he smells like. You know what he smells like, I said. I think it's his soap. Nan uses the same one as me and Robin but Grandad has his own soap. It's orange and it smells funny. You asked if we were having a nice time with Dad and I said

It's brilliant. You asked if I would like to live in South Africa all of the time but I said No and you said Why not? I said because I would miss Beth. You didn't say anything and I said You don't like Beth, do you? You asked me why I thought that and I didn't know. You said of course you liked Beth, she was my friend and she had been really kind to me. I said I know, that's why I like her. You said I know. I told you that Beth sometimes nicks stuff from the shop near the bus stop. Then I felt a warm fuzzy feeling and I woke up. The sheets were wet and sticking to my legs and you weren't there.

Everyone was waiting for Zami to come back but he didn't. He didn't come and he didn't come. I didn't want to go on the tyre swing because I knew I wouldn't see Tonyhog, only his grave. Silumko came and Dad told him everything that happened. Zami didn't do anything wrong, I said, and Dad said I know that, Indy, I'm worried about him that's all.

I showed Nan how to play the drawing game even though she wasn't really interested. Picasso drew a restaurant. I knew what it was because of all the tables and chairs and a man in a chef's hat but I pretended not to guess so we broke our record of forty non-stop guesses. I knew Picasso wasn't you. It was just some random person.

Robin said Maybe Zami could be at his sister's house. I wanted to go there but Dad said he didn't know where she lived. I told him I could remember the journey and I begged for us to go. In the end Dad said Okay. When we got in the car I didn't look towards the end of the garden where Tony's grave was but I knew it was there. There was a pile of earth next to the fence where we made it.

A new security man was standing in front of the gate instead of Lindisizwe. We drove the same way the bus went. Dad was amazed I could remember the journey but it was easy. Normally when we are driving anywhere the thought of arriving makes me feel so tired I feel like I could sleep for a hundred years like a princess in a fairytale but this time I was urgent to get there. We parked in the marketplace and everyone was looking at us. Some children came up and were touching the car. Dad said We mustn't be long. We knocked on the door with the number painted on it. Zami's sister was wearing the same skirt as last time, with her baby asleep in a towel wrapped around her again. Dad asked if she had seen Zami but she said no. She was a bit nervous and she only opened the door a tiny little bit. Dad was speaking in his kind voice that annoys me when he speaks like it to me but I was glad he was speaking like it to her. He said If you see your brother, can you tell him to contact me as soon as possible? Tell him he's not in any trouble. Then something moved in the dark at the back of the little room and Zami came out of it. He stood next to his sister and said something to her in his foreign language. She opened the door a little bit more. Zami had a cut on his eye, all shiny and red. I told him

Tonyhog was dead and that we made a grave. I said When are you coming home but he didn't say anything back. He was looking at Dad with his big round eyes, one of them with a big cut right next to it. Dad said That wound looks nasty, why don't you come home and let Silumko take a look at it? Then Dad spoke some African to him and Zami spoke in African back.

I said to Dad What about you-know and Dad said to Zami Indigo wants to know if your sister would like to come and live with us. You can have my room, I said to her, and Dad said the baby could come too. Zami didn't say anything and nor did Nomsa but she took Dad's hand and pressed it against her forehead. Dad said I think we should go now and we went inside the house to get Nomsa's things. She didn't have many.

There were lots of people standing next to our car when we came back to it – grown-ups as well as children. We didn't talk to them, we just ignored them. It felt like bad manners but we didn't know them, even though they were touching our car. It was burning hot inside so we had to switch the aircon to max. Nomsa and Zami sat in the back like me and Robin. I sat in the front like a grown-up.

Actually, I don't think I will go to the girls' school, I said. I think I will go back to England with Nan and Grandad. Dad didn't say anything. Nan and Grandad are good at looking after me and Robin, I said, and we are English not African. Dad still didn't say anything and I wondered if he was listening. I wondered if I would have to say it all again but then he stopped the car on the side of the road and switched off the engine. What does Robin think, he said, and I said You'll have to ask him. Good answer, Dad said. He thinks the same as me, I said. We want to go to the same school and it would be better for us to stay in England with people we know. Our friends are at school and our neighbours go to the same school, like Beth. No one spoke for ages. Zami and his sister were just sitting in the back looking at nothing and me and Dad were in the front looking straight ahead at the long empty road in front. Dad's eyes had tears in them but he wasn't crying. He said even though he was disappointed he understood. He leaned over to me and we hugged with our seatbelts stretching. I told him he would have Zami and Nomsa to keep him company. And Beautiful, too. I could smell his smell and I breathed it in to keep it. Me and Robin can save up all our birthday and Christmas money so we can come out every holiday, I said. He laughed at that and I knew it was because a plane ticket is more expensive than pocket money. I know it's expensive, I said, and he said Indigo you are turning into a mature young woman and it is lovely to see. I am proud of you. Then he started the car engine again.

He said had I thought of writing down some of my thoughts and I thought he meant about whether to stay in South Africa or live in England but he meant about everything else. About you. I said What's the point and he said No point but it might make you feel better.

He said Maybe you could write Mum a letter, tell her how you feel. He said That's what mums are for. She's dead though, I said. You can't write a letter to someone who's dead. I looked out of the window. Dad didn't say anything for a long time and I thought how when I got back to Dad's I would get some of his Taylored Travel writing paper to write it on because you are Karen Taylor and I am Indigo Taylor and I love you.

We were driving back to Dad's house and we overtook a bus like the one me and Robin and Zami rode in, all smelly with loud music and rough driving. I looked to see if I could see us in it. I imagined Robin and me on the bus and it made me think about the journey home to England when all of this will be over. It will be winter there and all the shops will still have their Christmas decorations up even though my legs are quite tanned. I don't know if it will be day or night by the time we get there and I'm not sure if Grandad parked his car at the airport or if we will get a taxi. If we get a taxi, Robin will sit in the front and I'll go in the back all squashed up with Nan and Grandad, so close I will be able to smell Grandad's horrible soap. The driver might have his radio on. He'll drive us and Nan will show him where to stop. If it's Grandad driving he'll know where to stop. If it's Grandad driving, he'll park the car in the drive and when we get out and get our bags he'll lock all the doors then check them, testing the handles to make sure they really are shut. It will be freezing cold, with frost on the grass. Everyone will shiver and Grandad will say Brass monkeys. Nan's got the keys on her teddy bear keyring and she'll say Home Sweet Home as she opens the door. If it's late at night she'll say it in a quiet voice. Minnie will start barking next door and wake everyone up and Beth will have to whisper in her ear that it's okay, she doesn't need to protect her because it's just us getting home from holiday. She'll be in bed in her heart pyjamas but Minnie will run to the door barking so she'll have to get up and cuddle her and tell her that everything's fine. She'll scraggle her ears and wave her paw up at the window. I'll wave back and Nan will tell me off and say You can see Beth tomorrow. The house will smell of emptiness. It's not big or luxury like Dad's. The front room will look really small. Robin will go straight to the toilet and Grandad will moan that he's going to be in there for ages. Nan will say Doug leave him be and get that kettle on. I'll say I'll make the tea and Nan and Grandad will look at each other and think like Dad that I am growing into a mature young woman but I'll pretend I don't notice and I will just carry on. I'll fill the kettle and I'll have to plug it in because Nan will have taken all the plugs out while we've been away, then I'll take four cups and put four teabags in. While we're waiting for the water to boil Grandad will smile at me in a shy kind of way and call me by my name and tell me it's a small life but it's a good life.

Acknowledgements

THANK YOU, Holly Ainley, for your sensitive and thoughtful editing, and for the tender feeling you have shown my characters.

I am grateful to Vicky Blunden for inviting me into the Myriad fold and to Candida Lacey for giving me such a warm welcome.

Thank you to those people who read early drafts of the novel and who provided support and encouragement: Stefania Mastrorosa, Maria Tilyard, Juliet Mushens and Sinead Keegan, as well as the students and tutor in Adam Baron's writers' workshop at Kingston University, winter 2010.

Especial thanks to my trusted first reader, PV (aka Polar Bear).

Thank you, Mum and Dad, and thanks to the rest of my family, too, for being there when I need you.

Finally, thank you to my three favourite people on the planet: Bosie, Alvy and Ned, for the faith you have in me and for the ways in which you love me.

MORE FROM MYRIAD EDITIONS

MORE FROM MYRIAD EDITIONS

MORE FROM MYRIAD EDITIONS

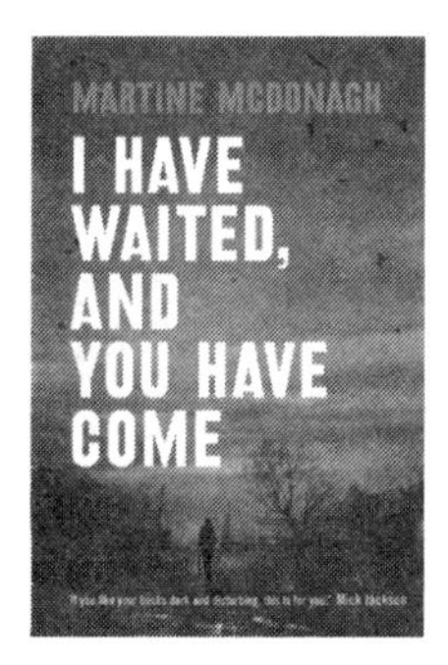

MORE FROM MYRIAD EDITIONS

HANNAH VINCENT began her writing career as a playwright. She is the author of plays including *The Burrow, Throwing Stones* (Royal Court) and *Hang* (National Theatre Studio). She studied drama at the University of East Anglia and has an MA in creative writing from Kingston University, London. Previously a BBC television script editor, she now teaches creative writing for the Open University and is studying for her PhD at the University of Sussex. She lives in Brighton.